Getting Hurt

ANDREW DAVIES

METHUEN

First published in Great Britain 1989 by
Methuen London
Michelin House, 81 Fulham Road, London SW3 6RB
Copyright © 1989 by Andrew Davies

British Library Cataloguing in Publication Data

Davies, Andrew, *1936–*
Getting hurt
I. Title
823'.914 [F]

ISBN 0-413-15960-4

Printed in Great Britain by
Richard Clay Ltd, Bungay, Suffolk

GETTING HURT

ONE

Denial; despair; anger; bargaining; acceptance.

These are the stages you go through. I like logical stages, don't you? I used to like them. Offer subject to contract; survey; searches; exchange; completion. Red; yellow; green; brown; blue; pink; black. The Stations of the Cross. They get you in the car, they explain what they're going to do to you, they listen quite patiently to what you have to say about it, and then they go ahead and do it anyway. And so on.

How can I be ill when I feel so strong?

Denial, despair, anger, bargaining and acceptance are the stages that you go through when you are negotiating the breakdown of a relationship. It must be true, because I read it in an Open University social sciences booklet that Muriel was good enough to lend me. She thought it might help. And I was grateful to Muriel, and grateful to the Open University too, because it gave me a few laughs when I read it. Some people would call them bitter laughs, but it seems to me mean and picky to make qualitative distinctions about a good laugh. Angel's laughter, devil's laughter, all that. A good laugh is a good laugh; always welcome. A good sob, too. More of that later. So, yes, I was grateful to

5

Muriel and to the Open University, for the laughs, and for distracting me for at least twenty minutes from what I was going through at the time. Am still, I suppose. Which was, I suppose, is, I suppose, anger, denial, despair, and so on, all experienced in the course of what the Open University wittily calls the negotiation of a relationship breakdown.

It doesn't actually feel as if you're negotiating anything, does it? I don't think so. And I would be very interested to meet the poor bastard who works his way through the standard stages in the right order, thoroughly exploring his despair – I imagine them as a set of matching labelled cans – scraping out the last piquant, evocative morsels of congealed despair-jelly from the bottom of the can before moving on to the heady delights of anger. And then, later on, doggedly chewing his way through chunk after chunk of tough, fibrous bargaining, which is rather like biltong, or pemmican; going about for weeks and months with his mouth full of the wretched whiskery stuff; consumed with longing, not for the loved one, but the vanished pleasures, the wickedly delicious artificial highs of denial.

No, they don't come in sequence, not in my experience. They come thick and fast, sometimes two or three at a time, with other things mixed in as well. A good jolt of anger, say . . . I am warm as toast, feeling the blood surging merrily into my muscles, all the way down my arms into my fingertips, hardly time to appreciate it before I'm seized by a creative surge of denial, such a powerful, confident illusion that I feel like a Lord of the Universe; then she looks at me, or I remember how she looked at me, and I quite suddenly and violently experience something the Open University booklet had nothing much to say about, and which feels like being expertly left-hooked under the heart by someone who knows what he's doing; Mike Tyson, say . . . but *from the inside*. This may or may not be what the Open University means by despair, but I doubt it; the sensation is wholly physical, and leaves me incapable of speaking, or indeed breathing, for rather longer than is probably good for me. This is quite often followed by an invasion of what I think must be genuine despair, which I would not recommend to anyone. Physically it manifests itself as a mirror image of the effects of anger: a sensation of profound muscular weakness. I can look at the back of my hand, say, and watch it lose colour as the blood drains away from it (Where to? Not my brain, that's for sure) until it looks like the hand of a dead man. (I have seen one or two of those. I know what I'm talking about.) Mentally it takes the form of a series of banal but unanswerable questions: how am I going to get through the rest of my life? Or, more to the point, how am I going to get through the next five minutes? I don't know what you do, but my usual tactic is to pour myself a large Scotch, and with luck get into a session of imaginary angry bargaining, which can be rather fun once I'm in the swing of it, and can sometimes lead me back to my favourite stages – denial and anger – which are best experienced simultaneously, like port and stilton. And so it goes. *Acceptance*? Don't make me laugh.

And after a time I came to understand that this was what it had always been like. Really. At the level at which most of us expend most of our energy denying, as they probably say at the Open University. That *is* what it's always been like, isn't it? Right from the start. I mean, kicking around in the womb, waiting till your fingernails have grown or whatever, desperately frustrated, wanting to get out there and see what it's all about, mad, mad to get on with it; then that long, frantic, claustrophobic swim down the birth canal, batter your way out, arms and legs going like pistons, well that's how I remember it . . . and then suddenly there you are, out there, in it. You can't believe it. You despair of it. It makes you very angry. *That's* why babies cry. And if you're too thick to get the message on your own, they hold you upside down and hit you a bit until you do. Give you something to cry about. Mike Gibson, who has done his fair share of holding babies upside down and hitting them a bit, once told me that the initial response of many new-born babies to the world is not to cry about it but to piss on it. Not a modest trickle, but a proud, defiant silver arc, soaking everyone and everything in range. Now that I come to think of it, that was my son Joe's first contribution to the ongoing collective dialectic, before they hit him a bit and gave him something to cry about. I don't believe that this invalidates my point. It simply adds another item to the list, or possibly two: defiance and contempt. So there we are, right from square one: denial; despair; anger; defiance; contempt.

Bargaining comes later. Acceptance when you die.

All right then. I met her . . .

No, I don't think I'm ready for that yet. I don't think you are, either. It's not a question of *met whom*? It's still a question of *who* met her? as well. All you know about me so far is that I am probably of the male gender, as we say these days, that I drink a bit, read a bit, have a son called Joe, and that I seem to be in a bit of a state about something. You may also be forming the rapid conclusion that I am more than a little unbalanced, and not intelligent or self-aware enough to understand what is happening to me; which means that I am less intelligent and self-aware than you are, and hence hardly worthy of your full attention. Maybe a bit of a bore; maybe worse, a source of aggravation without any compensatory illumination. You would not be the first to think that. The latter, anyway.

I am in a bit of a state, I admit. But I continue to function. And I have no idea, obviously, whether I am less intelligent and self-aware than you are. But I do function. For example, I earn, or at least make, a good deal of money, probably a good deal more than you do, through the exercise of my intelligence, judgement and experience. Even insight, sometimes. I'm a solicitor. The firm in which I'm a partner is one of the two most prestigious practices in the town where I live. Perhaps slightly less prestigious than the other one, which boasts – and I don't use the word idly – some clients from the local pea-brained aristocracy. But known to those who know these things as the more effective outfit. People tend to come to us, or to me, really, when they actually want to get things done, as distinct from pissing about. I can work very fast, and go for the jugular when strictly necessary. People sometimes sit in my office and literally ask me to do that. 'I want you to go for the jugular on this one, Charlie.' They sit there in my large, quiet, tastefully decorated office and instruct me to go for the jugular. They want me, so to speak, to tear other people's throats apart, so that they can see all the money gushing out. And generally I am able to oblige.

Occasionally, too, I see clients who really have murdered other people, though never, so far, by tearing their throats out. They tend to use language quite differently – euphemistically, really – frequently invoking concepts such as 'liberty' and 'order', as in 'right out of order'. I prefer these clients as language users, but to be fair some of them are pretty dreadful people

9

too. And, it has to be faced, rather less honest than the other lot. Sometimes, though . . . sometimes more . . . interesting.

The town where I live and work is on the whole very pleasant to look at and walk about in. It was built, most of it, as a spa, in the Regency period, and continued to prosper as such throughout the nineteenth century; which means that the centre of it is full of handsome, well-proportioned, early nineteenth-century houses for smug bastards like me to have their offices in, and even bigger ones further out, in which my go-for-the-jugular clients live the lives of gentlemen. Beyond that it's farmers, serious farmers and joke ones, and horsey people. Quite a few of the people you see on television jumping over things on big horses live round our way. And come into town to avail themselves of our jugular service from time to time.

It's an old family firm. Not my family. I was invited in quite a few years ago when the senior partner realized that the practice needed an urgent brain transfusion. My name is Charles Cross, and people call me Charlie. I have no opinions about that. It seems to make them feel more comfortable.

I'm a big man: tall, and broad too. I used to be rather fleshy, but not too distressingly so. She liked it, and she always told the truth about that sort of thing, though not other sorts of things. I'm about a stone lighter now, and not really fleshy at all. Anger and despair, I suppose. Anger makes you too impatient and well . . . lively, to be bothered with eating very much. Despair depresses the appetite.

* * *

So my suits hang rather more loosely on me than they were wont to do. (I am, I'm sorry to tell you, the sort of man who wears suits.) I quite like the effect. Odd, how vanity seems to linger on. I look at myself in mirrors quite often – to see how I'm getting on. My hair is brownish, my eyes blueish. My nose is broadish and straightish. My chin is what people call strong, and I still have just the one. On the whole I think I look like a good, reliable, blokeish sort of bloke. Except that now and then, especially recently, I see this rather wild and dangerous expression on my face, as if someone else has moved in for a while without quite knowing what he's doing there, though I wouldn't want to be too melodramatic about it.

Physically I am very strong. People give me jars to open and heavy suitcases to lift on to racks, and I enjoy doing that sort of thing; actually sometimes I wish people would give me filing cabinets to hurl through first-floor windows. It has always puzzled me a bit, this physical strength thing, because I haven't done an honest day's physical work since I was twenty-five.

I am also quite light on my feet, quite dexterous. Good at games like tennis, which I still play a lot and still usually win at. I used to be passionately fond of dancing, of all things, and still imagine myself doing it. In my imagination I dance magnificently, terrifyingly, dancing it all out, the lot of it.

I am, I have been told, quite gentle. Clients find me easy to talk to, they say. Not just the property sharks with their jugular aspirations and the criminals whose liberty and sense of order have been interfered with, but the other ones, the ones I always think of as Ruth's clients; the poor, ordinary, bewildered, desperate sods

11

who come in and blurt out their messy lives across this desk, day in, day out. They say, some of them say, that I talk to them like a human being, not like a solicitor, and they are surprised when they see what I am like in court, doing my stuff. But these days, I often feel like blurting my own mess straight back at them. Which is why, perhaps, I'm sitting in my office now, at nine in the evening, drinking and smoking and talking into this machine.

I used to be married but now I'm not.

On the night when all this started . . . no.

I am walking up the stairs in my khaki shorts and my white T-shirt, in the late afternoon. I am staying with my parents in a boarding house on the Gower Coast, and my room is on the top floor. I climb the stairs three at a time, enjoying the stretch of it, feeling the air cool on my legs – the window on the landing is wide open – and smelling the cabbage cooking downstairs. I think I must be about eleven years old.

When I get to the landing on the top floor I see that the door to my room is ajar and I push it open and go in. At first I don't notice anything strange about it. The walls are painted white and the curtains and bedspread are yellow. The window is angled to catch the setting sun, so that the whole room glows with the yellow light.

The yellow dog is standing by the bed, waiting for me. It is a very big dog of a kind I have not seen before, its head broad and squarish, like a mastiff's. I stand in the

12

middle of the room staring at the yellow dog, and the yellow dog stands by the bed staring back at me. Then, slowly, it draws its lips back from its teeth and smiles at me. This smile makes me feel very uneasy, as though, in some way I cannot understand, the yellow dog and I are accomplices.

I would like to go out of the room, but I can't make my legs move. What I have to do is stand absolutely still in the centre of the room and wait while the yellow dog, still smiling, pads silently across the room to me. When he reaches me, he opens his jaws very wide and then closes them around my right thigh, very high up, near the groin. I can feel his teeth going through the flesh and it hurts very much indeed, worse than any pain I have felt before; but the yellow dog and I remain completely silent and motionless.

It goes on for a very long time. I can hear people talking downstairs and yelling from somewhere outside. I can even hear the sea in the distance. I can feel the cool breeze on my face from the window. I can still smell the cabbage cooking in the kitchen. But I cannot move or cry out. The yellow dog's teeth cut deeper and deeper into my thigh. It goes on for a very long time and it hurts very much indeed.

I feel very tired all of a sudden. I'm going to stop now. I'll start again tomorrow. Straight in tomorrow. Promise.

TWO

It was after twelve when they called me that night, the night I met Viola. I was duty solicitor. I had been doing more than my fair share of being duty solicitor for some time, what with Ruth leaving the firm and Laura leaving me. I didn't mind. I rather liked it, and it wasn't as if they often caught me tucked up and snoring in my pit. Not insomnia exactly: rather, that living on my own after so long living with someone else, I found it quite a problem knowing when it was time to go to bed, and discovered that I needed far less sleep than I'd always thought I needed. I'm not sure whether this is a good thing or not. At first it seemed like a definite plus factor, later not.

When the phone rang I was doing very little indeed. I was sitting in my chair in the flat staring rather vaguely at one of my Harry Holland's; the small one, the one of the chap sitting in his vest on the edge of the bed staring rather vaguely out of the window. The room in the picture is very sparsely furnished, as is the room in my flat. He has a table with a radio and a newspaper on it, and so do I. He may have other things, but that's all you can see of his room. Through his window he can see a hazy landscape, with low hills in the distance and two factory chimneys in the middle distance. Hence the haze, I suppose. From the light I judge it to be late afternoon, though I might be wrong about that. He looks to me as if he has been sitting there in his vest for quite some time, staring vaguely out of the window. It's a very calm sort of picture. I think what I particularly like about it is the dull, musing feel it has. I can never make up my mind whether he has recently woken up from his siesta, or whether he is trying to decide if it's time for a sleep. Or indeed both. I am pretty sure that he has no intention at all of getting dressed and going to work at the factory in the middle distance. Certainly not within the next couple of hours, anyway. I am – I used to be – perfectly content to sit there for an hour or so, musing sluggishly about the chap in the vest, staring vaguely at him while he stares vaguely out of the window. That's what I like about the picture. That and the colour of the bedspread, which reminds me of a blue dressing gown my mother once had. The picture is called 'Turin'.

Please try to excuse all this. I think it's called avoidance behaviour. And it may all, somehow, fit in.

The voice on the other end was a male voice, slightly breathy, and oddly . . . prim. He told me what his name was, and apologized rather elaborately for disturbing me at such a late hour. I said that that was all right. He said that he was visiting the area from the South West, and he had been advised that it was his right, and also in his interest, to contact a solicitor. Before I could break in and tell him that was fine and I was on my way, he went on to tell me that he had chosen my name from a list supplied to him at the station, that my name had indeed been recommended to him as a particularly sound choice. There was a sort of wheedling fulsomeness about the way he went on that I particularly disliked. So I told him rather brusquely that I'd be over in five minutes and I was sure we would get things sorted out for him. There was a short pause, and then a small, high, breathy titter from the other end (all right, sometimes I *am* mean and picky about laughter) and he said he didn't think that was very likely, but he was grateful all the same.

Then the station sergeant came on, which was odd in itself. He's a man I know quite well; Edgar is his name, and we usually call each other Edgar and Charlie, except in court of course. But this time he called me Mr Cross, and he went on about being sorry to disturb me and being very grateful as well; and then, as if he'd caught that prim, portentous tone off the other fellow, told me he was glad they'd drawn me, because this one was a little bit out of the ordinary, this one was something special. He sounded as if he was inviting me to his engagement party, or something.

My flat is in the middle of town, less than five minutes walk from the police station, and I have always rather enjoyed these short, nocturnal, urban strolls. The town at night is quite different in character. Very lively, in fact, especially between eleven at night and one in the morning. Despite its sedate image, it has always done surprisingly well in the violence statistics, and recently it has acquired a growing reputation as one of the most fashionable places to go for a fight, attracting carloads of chaps from as far as twenty or thirty miles away, who swarm along the elegant arcades and crowd out the handsome Georgian pubs (handsome from the outside anyway), drinking with grim determination until they become extremely brave and bad-tempered.

Then at closing time they swarm on to the streets, dressed in light summer clothing whatever the weather, which has always puzzled me – perhaps it helps them to feel more aggrieved if they are wet and chilly – and proceed to beat the shit out of each other. The town's response to this is to maintain what it calls a high police profile, which means, in effect, that the police field a gang as well, which comes in handy when the visitors fail to turn up, and facilitates a three-cornered fight when they do. Lately, some of the fights have been very nasty, involving the use of knives and other sharp implements, and even the odd death. I have to say that, despite my highly ambivalent emotional stance towards violence, I find all this deeply dispiriting. It's the randomness and the impersonal cruelty, I think. Getting together with three or four of your friends and kicking in the face of a single opponent, even if he has looked at or spoken to you in a grossly libertarian fashion, seems to me to involve such a degree of willed failure of the imagination . . . I once intervened in one of these events, being near enough and thus appalled enough, and also drunk enough myself. I put it to the aggressors, all of whom were wearing cotton shirts in pastel colours with little emblems depicting crocodiles over their left tits, that fair was fair and enough was enough, why not fuck off and leave the poor fucker be, and prepared myself to defend this modest proposal physically, by now wondering why the hell I had got myself into it. They asked me why I didn't fuck off myself and mind my own business, but then, to my surprise, seemed content to let the matter lapse into an ill-tempered but somehow lifeless exchange, during which they gradually drifted away, shouting abuse not at me, but at the poor fucker on the pavement, who, incidentally, seemed not particularly moved or grateful or even interested in my concern for his welfare. Of course, he was probably drunker than the rest of us put together. He got shakily to his fucking feet and fucked off in a determined but wavering fashion, leaving a wavering trail of blood; on reflection, I decided to fuck off myself.

They leave me alone, you see. Even when provoked. Sometimes, even in the thick of it, they find time to

17

shout a cheery if incoherent greeting as I pass. It's almost as if they recognize . . . no, that's ridiculous.

Avoidance, avoidance.

When I got to the police station, a quite repellent, exorbitantly expensive affair of mainly yellow bricks and glass – one of the few modern buildings in the town – I saw where all the police were; loafing by their cars and lurking about the foyer looking alert and gossipy. I went to see Edgar at the desk and he took me down to the cells (more tasteful, exposed brick, almost as nasty as that campus university you probably went to). While he was taking me down there he found time to tell me that my client had not been charged yet, but was being questioned about a rape he had certainly committed, a robbery they were thinking of forgetting about, and several more serious offences (*more* serious offences?) committed further afield; to wit, in Worcester, Taunton, Ross-on-Wye, a lay-by near the Strensham motorway services, and so on. At the moment there was a bit of a lull while they waited for some important people who were driving up from Cardiff and Bristol. So before they had extracted my client from his cell I had gathered that I was in for a chat with the M5 Monster, or, to put it more precisely, a man suspected of a series of sex crimes, three of them murders, committed in a variety of places between Birmingham and Exeter.

They put us in a very small yellow-bricked interview room and we sat down and had a look at each other. He saw . . . well, you know what he saw. I saw . . . well, at first sight I saw what I expected to see from the voice on the telephone. He looked like a smart, keen young rep, perhaps for sun-beds or jacuzzis (that sort of area anyway), who had had the bad luck to be done for driving over the limit when only marginally over and was shitting discreet, prim bricks because his job was on the line. He really did look as ordinary as that. Slight, shortish, early thirties, thin-faced, precise of speech. A snappy dresser, too. They had taken his tie and shoelaces away of course, but he still looked very smart in his close-fitting, double-breasted suit. (Crazed Solicitor asks Motorway Monster for Name of Tailor.) His face looked all right too; in terms of physical damage, that is. And he didn't move as if he had been hit. Edgar, as a matter of fact, runs a commendably tight ship, but boys will be boys. Though actually it's only the ones who do things to children or old women or policemen, or the ones who put bombs in pubs, that get seriously damaged in police stations as a rule. Or people suspected of those acts. Major sexual offenders who do final and terrible things to adult women tend to get treated, not exactly like cut crystal, but with something like the awed respect evoked by especially delicate and valuable works of art. Not very nice, is it? But if someone had been watching us they might have said that that was the way I was looking at this chap. My client.

He was actually, I realized, rather good-looking in his petite way. Small, neat, straight features, neat short hair. Bright brown eyes with long lashes. A mouth that you might describe as sensitive; I might myself. Even before we started to talk, I had the naïve thought that this guy was quite attractive really; he would probably appeal to women, some women anyway, enough women, so what was he doing all these other things for? Silly. Because we know that's not the point at all, don't we?

*   *   *

19

The next thought I had about him, while I was outlining his present situation and the options available to him (which were not many), was what fine bones he had. Very thin-looking wrists. Very delicate cheekbones. I felt that if I took his face in my hands – he had a small face and my hands are very large – I could crush it like an empty lager can. I don't know why I felt that. It rather took me by surprise, and made my exposition of his current situation less masterly than it might have been.

While I was talking to him he sat very still, nodding from time to time in an alert, perceptive sort of way, like a good student trying to impress his master. But every now and then he glanced up at me in quite a different way, almost as if he was . . . flirting. I didn't like that. Would you like that? It made me feel very uncomfortable, and it also reminded me of someone . . . I couldn't think who it was. I didn't even know whether it was a man or a woman, which was very disconcerting.

I told him what was likely to happen to him. Assuming that he wasn't released, he would be charged, and remanded in custody for seven days, and the case would be committed to the Crown Court. We would enter no pleas at this stage, but I would take his instructions and apply for legal aid. A bail application would be pointless at this stage, but we might consider trying it on later. In the meantime, all I could advise him was to say as little as possible. At this point he treated me to another of his flirty glances.

'I'm sorry if this makes things difficult for you, Mr Cross,' he said. Bashful. That was how he looked: bashful. 'But I'm afraid I've been talking to the police quite a lot already. They were very courteous, one in particular seemed quite sympathetic. I'm afraid I couldn't help myself.'

'Have you signed any statements?'

'I'm afraid I have, yes, Mr Cross.'

'And what you've said . . . incriminates you?'

He nodded. Looked up. Flirty. Bashful schoolboy. 'I'm afraid it does, yes.'

In a strange way he looked quite proud of himself. I realized that I was beginning to feel rather odd: cold and sweaty. I wanted to take a little rest from this; I wanted to get out of the yellow brick room.

'Well, it might be possible to limit the damage,' I heard myself say in a hollow, hearty voice. 'We'll argue that the statements were involuntary. You weren't allowed immediate access to a solicitor; you may well have been questioned too long, so that you were exhausted and confused. We'll see what can be done along those lines.'

'But you see, Mr Cross, I'm not quite sure that I do want to limit the damage,' he said. And then he looked up and flashed me this really horrible smile, terrified and dangerous both at the same time. The kind of smile a dog gives you just before it bites you. And I realized who it was he had been reminding me of.

'I am guilty, you see.' The smile again. 'Aren't we all?'

If I had been on anything like normal form I would have given him a cheerful but brutal reminder that I was the solid citizen and pillar of the community here, and that he was the chap who was looking at several concurrent or indeed consecutive life sentences, and that existential notions of universal guilt seemed just a little bit inappropriate; a bit of a joke in poor taste in the circumstances, didn't he think? But somehow I didn't feel like saying any of that just then. Instead I advised him to think things over very carefully and to try not to make any more confessions for the time being. Meanwhile I would go and have a chat with the investigating officers and try to find out what course of action they had in mind. I wouldn't leave the station until he had been formally charged, and he was to be in no doubt that everything possible that could be done for him would be done for him. The sweat was running down my back by now.

'Thank you very much, Mr Cross,' he said. 'I'm sure you'll do your best.'

I turned round at the door to say cheerio, or see you later. Make some sort of human signal.

He was doing the smile again.

'How can I be ill when I feel so strong?' he said.

I hung around the station for another couple of hours, by which time I didn't have a client any more, to my considerable relief. They took him off to Cardiff and charged him there, and lumbered some poor Welsh bastard with him. Mike Gibson had been hanging round the station as well. He moonlights as a police doctor and I often run into him down there. Usually it's when one of my jugular or horsey clients has been pulled in for drunken driving and Mike's been taking the blood samples. On this particular night he'd been collecting saliva and semen samples as well, and I thought he looked a bit pale as we stood in the car park watching the cars – there were four or five of them – taking my ex-client away. It wasn't really cold out there but I did notice him shiver briefly. Somehow I didn't fancy walking back to the flat just yet, but what else was there to do?

'Fancy a drink?' he said. He'd never suggested that before, not at that sort of time.

'Is there anywhere?' Drinking in pubs and clubs in our town is largely the prerogative of customers who have not yet reached the legal age for drinking in pubs and clubs. I knew that one vile disco at least would still be serving, but he could hardly be proposing a visit to one of those. Or inviting me to his place. Mike hates his home and spends as little time there as possible. I hoped he wasn't thinking of my flat. But he wasn't.

'I know a place,' he said. 'Guido's.'

Then I remembered I'd heard of it; one of my clients had mentioned it, a Sikh chap who liked to think of himself as a professional hit man. Was one, I suppose, though it could hardly be described as a full-time job and he wasn't very good at it.

'It's all right,' he said. 'Quiet, anyway. And they serve drinks there.'

Guido's turned out to be a darkish, lowish, first-floor room. Decorated, not inappropriately for the hour and the mood, in various faded shades of blood-red and black. A couple of parkers standing up at the bar. I think they were plain-clothes policemen. One of them kept rubbing the side of his face with his left hand and then looking at his fingers. The other one spent several minutes trying to get his hand into his hip pocket, which was covered by a buttoned flap. Parkers do things like that. I like watching parkers. I still do like that. A woman of about forty with smudged lipstick was telling a long story about the misery of her current marriage to a gloomy, stoical-looking chap of about fifty. Three quiet Sikhs sat at a table in the corner with a bottle of whisky. There was no sign of anyone who might have been called Guido. The guy with the moustache who ran the bar seemed to be Polish or something, and so did the tall, dark, sullen-looking girl who carried the drinks to the tables. Yes, that was all I saw at first: tall, dark, sullen-looking girl.

* * *

We both seemed to need to talk a bit about my ex-client, but we had a little initial difficulty knowing how to go about it; I think that neither of us was sure whether we wanted to talk properly, or just be blokeish about it. Mike told me that the chap had been extremely apprehensive about the blood test: not anxious about tell-tale blood types or anything, just frightened and queasy about having the syringe stuck in his arm and seeing the blood come out.

'And then,' said Mike, 'when it was time for the semen sample, I asked him if he'd like anything to look at.'

'What d'you mean, anything to look at?'

'You know,' he said, impatiently. 'Wank-books.'

'You mean you carry them round with you for such occasions?'

'Yes, of course. Look, this isn't the point.'

'What sort?' I was very interested. This seemed to throw a new light on Mike in some way.

'*Christ*, Charlie! A representative *selection*.'

'Sorry,' I said, still wondering though. 'Do go on.'

'Well, he gave me this very affronted look, like Mrs Tabitha Twitchit, and said in this very headgirl way that he had no need of that sort of thing, thank you very much.'

Tabitha Twitchit and headgirl were not bad stabs at it; not quite right, but close. Of course, perhaps he had shown a different side of himself to Mike. I don't know why it seemed so important to know that, and it was, of course, impossible.

'The thing was,' said Mike after a moment, 'the thing was he took about ten bloody minutes over it. And I found myself spending those ten minutes trying to imagine . . . well, trying not to imagine, what he was thinking about.'

'Yes,' I said. I ordered two more large ones, and the tall, dark, sullen girl came over and smacked them down on the table. I had a vague sense that she was glaring at me, but I was more interested in what I wanted to say to Mike, who had, as it were, just given me permission to try.

'I got the feeling that he was . . . sort of flirting with me, though that's not quite the word.'

'Yes, I think I . . .'

'D'you know who he reminded me of? Charlie Chaplin. You know, that fine-featured, delicate sort of *fussy* face, and those quick little prim gestures, and sudden sideways glances at you to see how you're taking it; sort of *wheedling*. And that horrible, horrible smile. You know, wheedling you in, and then suddenly letting you have that smile, like a dog's smile. You know, just before he bites you? Does that make any sense?'

'Yes,' he said slowly. 'I didn't see it then, but I do now. Charlie Chaplin. Yes.'

'Amazing, isn't it? Here I've been all my life, rooting for W. C. Fields as the man who really said it all, and all the time it was that bloody little sentimentalist who . . . takes you nearest to the heart of darkness. Sorry.' I had got carried away and embarrassed myself a bit.

'No, no,' he said. 'I do know what you mean. Really.' He swallowed what was left in his glass. 'He was mad as a hatter, of course.' He was looking for a comfortable evasion, a route back to being blokes, and I didn't blame him. Mad as a hatter was nothing like it, nothing like it at all; we both knew that. Dog Smile, on his journey in the dark towards Cardiff and whatever was going to happen to him there. Hardly interested in what was going to happen to him because he'd already gone his journey, gone further maybe than he'd ever meant to. But he was still human. He was still taking a little bit of us with him. Us blokes.

Yes, I know, I *know*; what is much more to the point about him is that he interfered with, catastrophically interrupted the lives of several young women who were simply walking about the world without the faintest idea of what was going to happen to them; ended the lives of three of them in ways that make me feel sick when I try to imagine them – yes, I think I *can* imagine what it feels like to be utterly at the mercy of someone stronger than me who wants to hurt me very much; I'm not trying to drum up *sympathy* for Dog Smile, for Christ's sake, I'm just trying to understand; it's not as if I fucking well *enjoy* all this, you know . . . sorry.

It's just the strangeness of both things happening on the same night, as if . . . sorry.

'Let's have a bottle of champagne,' said Mike Gibson.

I thought that was a terrible idea, and said so.

'No, no,' he said. 'It's a brilliant idea. It's just what we need. A little defiant gaiety. Magic, after spirits. Trust your medical man.'

'No, I'll just have one more Scotch and then lurk off, I think,' I said.

'Please,' he said. 'To please me. Let's give that girl a bit of a surprise. Just for badness?'

'All right then,' I said.

'That's a good boy,' he said. 'You know, you need a bit of being taken care of; you know that? You're a bit of a wounded soldier, you are.'

'And you can fuck off with your bedside manner,' I said, feeling in fact deeply moved by the tenderness of his tone, faked or not. I think that both of us had put away at least a couple of big ones before we'd been called out to see Dog Smile.

The dark girl seemed utterly unimpressed by Mike's extravagant order, but she brought the bottle and two glasses over to the table, scowling rather theatrically, and this time I looked at her properly. I had had a vague impression that she was thin and rather frail; but there wasn't anything frail about her. She walked over to us with a long, springy stride; rather clever of her, I thought, what with all the tables and chairs cluttering the place up. She banged the bottle and the glasses down and stood there staring at us, as if defying us to ask her to pour it out. I had thought of her as sullen-looking, but close to she looked fierce rather than sullen; fierce and bright and sparky. And older than I'd imagined: late twenties, at least. I had the sudden thought that she and I could do each other harm. I'm not trying to be clever or anything: that was the way the thought presented itself.

Mike must have been impressed in some way as well, because he asked her if she'd like to join us and help us drink it.

'The office is closed,' she said abruptly.

'What?' he said. He seemed completely thrown.

'The office is *closed*, it's too *late* to talk to you, I don't *want* to talk to you, please drink your champagne and go home. You understand? The office is closed.'

She's mocking him, I thought. She glanced briefly at me, to see whether I appreciated her performance. I smiled at her. She kept a straight face, but I thought her eyes smiled a bit. Then she looked back at Mike.

'Well, look . . .' he said, rather helplessly, for him.

'Look what?'

'Do you like champagne?' I asked her. All I wanted was to prolong this for a bit, keep her this near for a bit while I looked at her.

'Of course.'

'Well, why not have a glass? You don't have to talk to us. You don't even have to sit down. You can take it over behind the bar and drink it there.'

She looked at me properly then. She frowned and bit her lip. I had the feeling that this was all in code, and that she was genuinely trying to make a very important decision. Then her face cleared. 'OK,' she said in a bright singsong. She turned on her heel and strode off to the bar and got another glass, and strode back to the table with it. I was aware of the three Sikhs watching all this with great interest.

We all watched her carefully fill the glass. When she finished, she looked up and grinned. It was a lovely grin, I thought. Very merry. Very cheeky. I was sure she was going to change her mind and sit down with us. And I think she saw that in my face. Then she turned round and went off back to the bar.

And that was it. We drank the rest of the bottle, and Mike told me something of the pleasures and problems of the woman he was seeing at that time. I listened to him and looked at her, moving about behind the bar. She looked over once or twice, but it was too dark to see her expression at that distance. We could do each other harm, I was thinking. We could do each other harm.

THREE

I DRINK A BIT, as you know. I also smoke a bit. Well, more than a bit. All right, I smoke a lot. I buy them two hundred at a time, extra mild ones these days, because I smoke so many of them that the ordinary sort hurt my throat. I buy them two hundred at a time, but I still seem to have to go to the shop a lot. When I notice I'm smoking, I enjoy it. Generally, of course, I don't notice. Sometimes I find I have two going at the same time, one in my fingers or in my mouth, another burning away in the ashtray over there, on the table, under the Harry Holland. Because I don't notice it, I don't mention it often. But if you want to picture me, picture me smoking. I was smoking when I was talking to Dog Smile. I didn't offer him one because I knew he wouldn't be a smoker. I nearly always get that right about people. I was smoking in Guido's. I'm smoking now.

Sometimes I try to restrain myself in company, but on the whole people have to put up with it. She liked it. She said it was part of my smell. And she was always truthful about that sort of thing, though not other sorts of things.

A few years ago, about the time of the worst of the bad patches with Laura, I met this girl. Woman. She was tall and dark and very frail-looking and serious. She had very white skin, that kind they call translucent, so that at the temples, for example, it had a bluey sheen under the surface. I felt very delicate and tentative about touching her. Her hair was black; thick and long and glowing. She had a full, wide mouth. What I really want to say about her face, her wonderful big, dark, serious eyes, etc, is that I could feel just from looking at her that she was capable of immense tenderness, and I felt such tenderness for her; not only felt it, but felt capable of expressing it, doing it, being it, more fully than I'd ever managed before.

We were in a clearing in the middle of a birch wood, and we were sitting looking into each other's eyes, and I was holding her thin white hand in my hand. What we were sitting on was a long and rather graceful ottoman, covered in dark blue Dralon. I am unable to explain this detail. I was talking, mostly, and she was listening. Listen, I kept saying, listen, and she listened to me. I told her all my stuff, the lot of it, because I could tell that none of it was going to bore her or baffle her; she could understand it all, she could handle it. And I told her about the tenderness I felt we could have together, and how much I loved her. She listened to all this very seriously and tenderly. She didn't laugh once. (I rather suspect, now, that she had no sense of humour at all.)

When I had finished telling her all this, she looked at me very tenderly and sadly. Then she told me, 'You came too late. I could have loved you, but I can't love you.' I was shattered. I felt as if my heart had stopped. I asked her what she meant, why couldn't she love me? And she said it was because I was in love with death.

When I woke up next morning I was still so powerfully in the grip of this dream that I threw all my cigarettes away and gave up smoking for good. It was horrible. I developed this disgusting phlegmy cough and felt sick and dizzy all the time. I gave myself a bad time and I gave everyone else a bad time, especially Laura. As the months went by, I began to feel marginally better, though only marginally. I yearned and craved with a double yearning and craving, and I felt so angry with her. Not Laura. I didn't tell anybody why I had given up cigarettes, that I was waiting for that girl, that woman, to show up. It was so fucking absurd.

And then one afternoon, about nine months after the dream, I was sitting in a cinema in London, having a couple of hours to spare before seeing a client who was up at the Bailey. *Tess of the d'Ubervilles* it was. Yes, maybe Nastassia Kinski had something to do with it. Anyway, I suddenly thought, fuck it, she's not coming, went out to the foyer, bought myself a packet of Benson's, and I've been at it ever since.

I thought it was a dream about smoking, you see. Now I think I might have got it all wrong.

The day after Dog Smile, I spent the morning in court. I was contesting a custody case, one of those I'd inherited from Ruth. I got a very good result, though not better than I was expecting. I'm afraid it was probably better than the result Ruth would have got. Despite her experience, she is still so nice and so principled that it often takes her by surprise; the way people get with each other, the lengths they will go to. The firm she has gone to now, they are all more like her. Their clients, virtually all of whom are on legal aid, think Ruth and her colleagues are wonderful, caring people, which they are, but they don't get very good results out of them. Patronizing bastard, eh? Yes. No doubt. But there is no point in not being honest. Ruth is a good person, a better person than me. But if you need a solicitor you would be better off with Charlie Cross. Ask anyone.

Faith Cracknell was in the chair. She knows me quite well and has always liked me rather than otherwise, being not averse to a laugh, but very irritable with time-wasters. The other side's solicitor was a petulant little fellow with verbal diarrhoea, and a way of pronouncing the word 'behaviour' that clearly got up Faith's nose. What he did was to drop the aitch and turn the final syllable into 'yah!' After a while I could see Faith's mouth tighten every time he said it. On such details are the fates of children decided.

No, there was more to it than that, to be fair. He, or his client, had decided to take a highly confrontational stance, dragging in absolutely everything that came to mind, which resulted in a tedious and rather spiteful-sounding catalogue of trivial whines and grouses. A lot of these involved disputes about who was supposed to collect the kids from school and when, and he got his times mixed up, which I had to point out. Regretfully, of course. Then we had a diverting passage about whether my client had forced Mark's nengles down the children's throats. Meanwhile, I was pursuing the other line, the high-minded, conciliatory one; two very caring and committed parents, virtues as well as faults on both sides, etc. Just as Faith Cracknell was beginning to look a little bored, I let drop the two ripe ones I'd been saving up. Regretfully, of course. Almost reluctantly. One of them was about destroying a healthy young cat (Faith Cracknell is very fond of cats, as I am). The other was a particularly striking couple of sentences from a letter. (I would not like to hear some of my letters quoted in court.)

* * *

So I got my result. I used to love winning so much. I still did then. Even now, I can get back into the feeling. Nothing to beat it. (Oh, but there is, there is.)

And all that time I was thinking about the girl in Guido's. Well, no, not thinking about her. She was just there, moving about quietly in the background, and every so often she would look over, but it was too dark to see the expression on her face.

In the afternoon I shifted a lot of paperwork. Two nursing home jobs. Nursing homes and rest homes are all the rage round here. Most of us will be in them before very long. Do you fancy that? Are you looking forward to it? No, neither am I. But I'm doing something about that. Just whisky and cigarettes, so far, mostly. Meanwhile, I process the paperwork. They're as near to a guaranteed certainty as you can get these days, nursing homes. You don't even have to see any old people if you don't want to. There are two ways of doing it: you can do an economy model for the DHSS standard rate. Or you can go upmarket. This barrister acquaintance of mine had a lot of time on his hands, as many barristers have, and a young woman with no job, but with a little house worth, say, seventy grand, on a mortgage, naturally. So they blew in his flat and her house and made a successful offer of two hundred and thirty thousand for this big Victorian country house. Borrowing nearly all the money, of course.

But they were still forty grand light on the deposit, and asked me if I'd like to come in for a bit, as a third partner. We dawdled a bit on exchange of contracts, so that we had planning and Health Authority permission through before completion; which meant that the merchant bank came through with the money on time, enough for the conversion as well. But the conversion never went ahead, because with all the plans and permissions and the lively state of the property market just then, the house was now worth nearly half a million. In fact we sold it for four hundred and seventy thousand, making eighty thousand clear profit each. Leaving out the legal fees. Amazing, isn't it? And you don't even need any money to do it. The barrister's very clever young woman was on the dole at the time, and getting assistance with her mortgage. They're doing the whole thing again now, but of course they don't need me this time. Except for the paperwork.

So there you are. Why don't you give it a whirl yourself? Perhaps you are, for all I know. What do you do about living in this desperate country? I do my stuff, as I did on the day after Dog Smile, and I write occasional large drunken cheques to Oxfam, and the Dog Rescue place, and the Cats' Protection League. Not all that large, though. Not all that often.

And that night I . . . no.

I used to believe in personal relations, as they say at the Open University.

She was there all the time, that afternoon, moving quietly about in the background.

Listen, I said, listen.

I felt that we could do each other harm.

FOUR

SOMETIMES CHOICES MANIFEST themselves as choices; more often, with me, they don't. I was loafing around in the flat again that night, vaguely thinking about the end of *Gulliver's Travels*. You know, when he finally gets back from his travels and he can't bear to see, touch or smell his family, and prefers the stable with its clean straw and the company of the horses. And everyone thinks he's mad, but they treat him very patiently, and eventually he gets back to normal . . . no doubt the Open University sees that as an unequivocally happy ending. I've never been able to make my mind up. I thought I might as well go to bed, so I got up; but instead of going into the bedroom I went out of the flat and walked down to Guido's.

She was there again. I would have felt bloody silly if she hadn't been there, but she was there, and what I felt was a genuine sick lurch. I felt as if I was leaning over the edge of a cliff. I felt . . . in jeopardy, and my head felt cold and weak. I told myself that this was stupid, that I was simply a bloke who had dropped in for a drink, and I sat down at a table.

There were other people there, about the same number as the night before, but I didn't look at them. I was waiting for her to walk over to the table. She'd seen me the moment I came in, but she took her time about coming over. She was moving about quietly behind the bar, doing nothing very useful that I could

35

make out, and every so often glancing round the room, but missing me out every time she did it. I liked this because it made me special. It was too dark to make out her expression at that distance, but I was sure that she was smiling. Normally I become extremely jumpy and irritable when I am not served quickly, especially with alcohol, but that night I was content to sit there at the table, waiting and smoking, while she played this game. Then she seemed to make her mind up, turned and looked straight at me, and walked over to the table. Same quick, springy stride.

I felt the thing again. An empty lurch. As if there were a hole in me that she could somehow fill. (Yes, I know, they could have a really good time with that one at the Tavistock Clinic, but that's how it felt.)

'Hello,' she said, as if I'd done something rather witty, coming here two nights running. I managed to say hello back, and then heard myself ordering a bottle of champagne, which I had not meant to do at all.

'Whole bottle? Just for you?'

'Yes, I could cope,' I said. 'I'd like it if you had a glass or two, though.'

She looked at me, frowning a bit, as she had the night before.

'You don't have to sit and talk to me or anything; you can take it over there if you like.'

She grinned. 'OK.'

She walked over to the bar and came back with the bottle and two glasses. I had no idea what I would do or say when she came back. I had managed so far without making a total prat of myself, but . . . 'Listen,' I said, before she had even got the bottle open. 'I do want to talk to you. I've been thinking about you all day.'

She stopped what she was doing and looked at me. 'Oh, yes,' she said, as if she understood about all that. 'I know.' I had such a sense of being understood, of being known; it felt so intimate in that second, it was as if we'd both taken our clothes off or something. I felt she might go on and say, yes, I know, isn't it terrible, so have I, what are we going to do about it? But all she actually said was, 'Well, not tonight, if that's what you mean.'

'No, I know,' I said. 'Sometime, though.'

She chewed her lower lip a bit. It's so strange, thinking back from now to then, those seconds when either of us could have made it different; the bubbles climbing back over the rim of the glass, the bottle tilting back upright, the wire coiling itself back into its neat plait, the scraps of silver paper rushing together to nestle round the cool green neck, me clumping backwards through the night streets, letting myself in, letting my jacket fall neatly on the back of the straight chair, collapsing backwards into the easy chair, my cigarette stub getting longer and longer as I stare vaguely at the man in the vest sitting on the edge of his bed staring vaguely out of the window . . .

'Look,' she said. 'I think you ought to know I'm sitting quite comfortably just now . . .' Then she grinned again. 'All right. I'll see you, if you like. Not tomorrow. Night after, this is OK for you?'

'Yes,' I said. Any bloody night was OK for me. 'Um, where would you like to . . . ?'

'In here,' she said. 'We'll have a drink. OK?'

'You mean you'll be working again, but this time you'll sit and have a drink with me?'

'No, I won't be working.'

'You wouldn't rather go somewhere else? We could go for a meal or something.'

'No,' she said. 'In here. We'll have a drink.'

'All right,' I said.

She poured a glass for me and a glass for herself. 'Thank you,' she said. For the drink? For thinking about her all day? For the invitation? Then she smiled at me.

'The office is closed now,' she said, smiling, and took her glass off behind the bar, where it was dark, and where she moved about quietly. I sat there smoking and watching her until I had drunk the rest of the bottle.

It isn't the sex, though that's part of it. It isn't love, or tenderness, though they are part of it too. It's the intimacy. That's what we want and fear. To be wholly known.

Did you ever go to one of those groups they had a few years back, that encouraged trust and intimacy and staying with the feeling and sharing the bathroom? In one of them I went to they had this sort of game. We sat on the floor in a circle, each thinking about the worst thing we'd ever done. Then, in turn, each of us went round the group, imagining confessing this worst thing to each person in turn; imagining how each person would react to it. And in doing this, realizing that what tormented each of us might well seem forgiveable, even trivial, to someone else. If that was how it seemed, and that was how it did seem to most of us, we were invited to take the risk of actually confessing this worst thing. And we did, most of us, take that risk. Including this woman, whom I had not noticed very much, except to think that she seemed rather nice, which is what I think most of us had thought about her. After looking round at each of us, what she felt able to take the risk of trusting us with was the following anecdote: a few years back, when her children were small, when she was in fact trapped in the house with a two-month-old baby, an eighteen-month-old toddler, and an older child of three or so, and three cats, one of the cats had done something to the baby; nothing appalling or permanently damaging – I forget what it was the cat had done in fact – but whatever it was, it had felt like the last straw to this woman; so what she had done was to pick up the cat, throw it in the oven, turn it up full, and leave it there. She left it there for two hours, during which time it had baked alive. This was the worst thing that she had done in her life, and this was what, after going round the group and imagining our reactions, she felt able to take the risk of sharing with us.

She had miscalculated our reactions of course. Every single person in the group reacted with horror and disgust. I regret to say that I did myself. I do regret it now; I feel ashamed. It wasn't just to do with my fondness for cats, which is on record, it was to do with the two hours she had left it there, after the spasm of rage and frustration or whatever it was. I just couldn't get my head round what she was thinking and feeling during those two hours, all those seconds in those two hours. I couldn't imagine and I couldn't identify.

It wasn't something *she* thought forgiveable or trivial. She was appalled and disgusted by it too. It was, after all, the worst thing that she had done in her life. But she had felt, after going round the group and imagining what our reactions might be, she had felt able to share with us the worst thing that she had done. She wanted to take that risk: to be wholly known.

But we have all done stuff, haven't we? What were they like, the people who found themselves in the position of being middle management in concentration camps? A bit like us?

It's a Friday lunchtime and I am in one of those big raucous pubs where all the bars have merged into one,

39

and everyone is yelling and shouting and laughing and interrupting everyone else; like those Belfast bars where there is always this hard edge over the usual pub noise, this urgency to get whatever it is said now, because the whole place might go up at any time, except that you can't believe it, you can't believe it's going to be today, because it never is. I'm just beginning to slow down and relax and accept and enjoy the decision that I knew was seeping up on me anyway, to ride with it and write off the rest of the week as far as work is concerned; I'm getting quieter as other people get louder, but enjoying it, the mingled accents and intonation and the whole orchestration of the place, and feeling that I am amongst friends who accept and like me, and savouring their individual essences, these friends of mine: Mike Gibson is here, and Steve is here, and Muriel is here, trying to explain what East Germany is really like, but no one will listen and pay proper attention to her; and bugger me, Brian Lewis is here too, a good friend of mine from school! I haven't seen him for years but it still feels exactly the same; he's sitting there grinning at me the way he did after the matches, in which he would always take two of them out and then get the ball away to me; he never wanted his name on the scoreline, just so long as we understood who had made it possible . . .

I can see and hear everything so clearly, every separate sound, including the jukebox, which I have not registered before except as an exhilarating background noise; but now I begin to notice that all the tunes it is playing are Irish rebel songs, and I begin to get a faint feeling of unease and wonder why my friends are not feeling the same thing that I feel; and I look at the men behind the bar and the men standing at the bar, and their movements begin to seem part of a planned, deliberate pattern. I am just beginning to formulate the idea that perhaps we should move the party on somewhere else, when the door opens and two quiet, friendly-looking guys come in, and they look around briefly and then move up to our table; one of them bends over Mike Gibson and begins talking to him quietly and seriously, and I can see Mike nodding and frowning, and nodding again, and he looks over towards me, sort of nodding in my direction, and the guy comes round to me and says in his soft friendly voice, 'Mr Cross, is it? You have to come with us now; this won't take long.'

And I look at my friends round the table and understand that this is something that I have to do, something I am needed for, and no one else will do; and it is good to feel necessary in this way, even though there is this faint vague corner of apprehension in it. I go out with the two quiet friendly guys into the car park, where the sun is shining after rain; it smells so fresh. They have an old Cortina out there and one of them gets into the driving seat and the other gets into the back seat with me, which I think is odd, but friendly too, and we drive out into the countryside; as we drive along they explain what they have to do, and what they have to do is to shoot me through the kneecaps. They explain this very considerately and quietly, as if they understand that this is bad news that they are breaking. The driver has fair curly hair and the back of his neck is burnt brick-red, as if he has spent much of his life working in fields or on building sites. Every so often he turns his head to smile at me. It's not a nasty smile or a cruel smile; he seems to want to reassure me that everything is as it should be. The other one, the one who does most of the talking, has a swarthy, gypsyish face and curly black hair, and a gentle soft voice with a little burred catch to it that suggests long nights of cigarettes and whiskey, and makes me feel close to him. He reminds me of one of those priests, the kind who always have a tab on the go and put something on a horse three times a week, and I feel like asking him if he ever contemplated the priesthood, and then feel like

41

giggling hysterically because I am, of course, very
frightened indeed.

Trying to keep my voice as calm, level and friendly as I
can, I explain to the swarthy man that there must have
been a mistake; I have nothing to do with them and
their struggles, I don't know the ins and outs of them;
that, while random violence shocks and depresses me,
I can understand that there is more than one view to be
argued; that I like and enjoy the company of his fellow
countrymen, that I have a good reputation amongst
them as a useful fellow to have about you if it comes to
a court case; that I don't even tell Irish jokes; that they
have, in fact, through some unfortunate failure of
communication, got the wrong man.

The swarthy man listens patiently to all this as if he has
heard it, or something like it, many times before. He
tells me that what I say may very well be true, in which
case he is sorrier than he can say, but it is not the issue.
The issue is that he and his friend have a job to do, and
without being melodramatic about it, it would be more
than their lives were worth if they let me go now. He
reassures me that he likes me, he likes the way I have
about me, that I seem a very good sort of man to him,
and that there is nothing personal about this at all.
Then he reminds me that this is not the end of the
world, sure it's nothing like that, that I'll walk again,
though naturally not as well as before. He has had a lot
of experience in these things, and if we all stay very
quiet and calm and steady, I can trust him to do a nice
clean job and not cause me any unnecessary suffering.

We are driving in country lanes now. Past the driver's
red neck and curly fair hair I can see the dark hedges,
the trees arching over, the bright patterns of sunlight

42

and shade. The driver's window is open and the smell of cut grass mingles with stale cigarettes and oil and the sour smell of my sweat. We are going quite slowly. I think about opening the door and rolling out into the ditch. The swarthy man is not holding a gun on me, though I am sure he must have one in his pocket. I imagine the bump of my shoulder against the door, tucking my head in to hit the gravel with my shoulder, up and running before they're out of the car . . . I cannot move. I cannot feel the muscles in my legs at all. My head feels very cold and still. I feel terribly resigned about everything. It is something we are all part of, something that cannot be helped. It is tender and blokeish; we are all wounded soldiers.

The car leaves the road, squeezes through a farm gate, and bumps over tussocky grass. When the driver switches the engine off I can hear a blackbird singing. The driver comes round to my door and opens it. At first I cannot make my legs move, but he offers me his big red hand and helps me out. When I am out of the car and standing, he keeps hold of my hand, but not tightly; he holds my hand as if I were a child and he is looking after me. We stand there holding hands in the middle of this big empty field while the swarthy man gets the shotgun out of the boot and unwraps it. Then he walks over to us.

'I'm not going to tie you up or anything, because I know you're going to be a good sensible fellow,' he says. 'You've done fine so far, and I appreciate that. Now, all I want you to do is hold tight on to Kieran's hand and stand very still.'

FIVE

WHEN I WALKED into Guido's she was sitting at a table. She had picked one out in the middle of the room, though there were several free around the walls where it was darker and safer. Later, though not then, I wondered whether she had chosen that table, had chosen Guido's itself, because she was wary of me, because she felt as I felt, that we could do each other harm. But that was later. All I thought then was: *there she is.* And my legs felt weak and my heart hurt . . . and something else as well, a sensation I sometimes get when I see a dog with a bandage, as if the whole area between my balls and my anus were dissolving . . . I don't know what it is; something to do with fear, pity, tenderness? It is not a feeling that goes well with walking or indeed standing, and I think I sat down rather clumsily.

'Hello,' she said, smiling. It was a big smile with lots of teeth, a brave smile in a way and a little girl's smile; the way my daughter, my sweet Sal smiled at me that summer in Menorca, when I was trying to get the spines out of her foot, to show me she understood I had to hurt her. She was wearing a black dress that left her arms bare. Her arms looked thin and strong, and the hair in her armpits and on her forearms was black, like the hair on her head. She seemed to be wearing no makeup, but she had put on a pair of earrings made of bright red feathers. I thought they made her look more wild and dangerous and vulnerable than ever. Listen, I would like to describe her to you properly, her face, I mean. You are probably thinking she looked pretty silly with her hairy armpits and feathers in her fucking ears but I promise you . . . I will try, properly, later. Just think of someone who gives you this sort of bother down there, someone who could do *you* harm. Just for now. I want to get on, I don't want to start crying again.

'So what are we going to drink?' she said.

'Champagne again? Or something different? Whatever you like.'

'No, champagne is good for me,' she said. 'I'll get it.'

'Listen,' I said, 'you're not working tonight; let them wait on you.'

'They are too *slow*. They are all lazy bastards.' She made it sound like one word: *lazy*bastards, as if it were a rare species of insect, or a sexual orientation.

She stood up and ran to the bar, and came back, grinning, with the bottle and two glasses. As soon as she sat down I started to tell her about the girl in the dream that I had thought was a dream about smoking. She sat very still and listened to the whole thing very carefully without smiling or speaking.

Then she said, 'No, I think this was not a dream about smoking.' Then she opened the bottle and poured us a glass each.

'Listen,' I said, 'I don't know what your name is.'

'Viola,' she said.

Viola is a name which in its English version has always seemed to me excruciatingly ladylike and precious; I associate it with that woman in the Eliot poem, the one with the candles and the velleities . . . Dorothy Tutin territory, if you take my drift, and a no-go area for me. In its Polish version it sounded harsh and breathy and personal, like something people do to each other. I tried saying it that way myself, and she corrected me until I had said it to her satisfaction.

'I know your name, a customer told me,' she said. 'You are Mr Cross.'

'People call me Charlie,' I said.

She laughed. 'Like Charlie Chaplin?'

'Christ, no,' I said. 'Not that. Emphatically not.'

'Good,' she said. 'I hate that little bastard.'

I felt a sudden rush of joy and optimism: not only could we do each other harm, we had something in common. I suppose I must have been grinning all over my face, because she was smiling back at me.

What happened next, I am afraid, is that I started to blurt out all my stuff at some considerable length. The childhood and the adolescence, and the dreams, and how my mother threw herself off a bridge on to her head on the day I got married to spite me because she couldn't marry me herself (not strictly true, but the emotional truth for me), and the stuff about Laura, and the stuff about Sal and Joe, and the stuff about work, and the stuff about death . . . all my stuff. Listen, I heard myself going, listen, listen; and she listened. I am, believe it or not, a reasonably reticent bloke in normal circumstances, but that night, and always, always with her, I wanted to be wholly known. I didn't want to fuck about and be clever and calculating and charming. I do that for a living and it's not a problem at work. Not really. It used not to be.

I wanted her to hear all my stufff, and I really think she wanted to listen to it. She listened to it all, and unlike the girl in the dream, she laughed quite a lot at some of it. She laughed about the Taxi Driver Bloodbath in the Nottingham Hotel, and at Ardent Lover gets a Finger in his Eye, and at the tale of how I came to beat up Laura's filing cabinet. I just couldn't stop them coming;

46

they were tumbling out randomly, all my stories, all my stuff . . . discharging, I think they call it at the Open University. Boring Middle-Aged Provincial Solicitor Oppresses Helpless Beautiful Refugee with Story of His Life. 'I wanted to be Wholly Known,' he pleads. Bound over to keep his trap shut for the next thirty years, or life, whichever is the longer. But she seemed happy to sit there and take it.

'Listen, listen, you keep saying to me. It's OK, Charlie. I'm listening.' And I looked at her face and saw that she really was listening, and happy to be listening. That was how it seemed to me. But how do we really know anything about another person?

After a bit I managed to slow down and even ask Viola some things about herself. She answered them all, but very briefly. It wasn't that she was evasive. She was economical with the truth, in that useful phrase we have now. She chose carefully what she wanted to tell me. She didn't want to be Wholly Known, not yet.

She came from Katowice, 'The dirtiest town in Europe I think.' A mining town near the Czech border, the skies dark with coal dust by mid-afternoon. 'In your nose . . . what you call them . . . bogeys? Like *sticks of charcoal*.' A clever student at school but also something of a juvenile delinquent. 'Plenty going on across the border. Just little things, dope, Sony Walkperson, you know?' She told me about the Czech dog who meets the Polish dog on the border. What are you coming into my country for? says the Czech dog. Oh, you know, Levi, hi-fi, automatic washing machine, says the Polish dog. And what are you coming to Poland for? I am coming to learn how to bark, says the Czech dog.

* * *

47

There had been nothing to do in Katowice except studying, skiing and fucking. (When she said fucking I felt weak again.) She had started an on-off affair with a lecturer from England when she was fourteen and had married him and come to Britain at nineteen. 'Not a passport deal. Just a bad mistake, you know.' She had tried going back, but felt foreign in both countries now. She had started a degree in philosophy at the local university, but she was disappointed in the teaching and in her fellow students, though she intended to press on. 'I think with this crap degree maybe I'll get a really flash job, DHSS even!' She said it so earnestly that I thought she was serious, until she grinned. She was getting no maintenance grant, so she drew social security and did two jobs, the one at Guido's and also some technical translation; she had fluent Russian and medium crap German, good enough for those nanas who paid peanuts for her time. 'And so, there I am, you see, all fucked up and nowhere to go!'

But she said it so merrily.

I wanted to hear all of this, anything, anything about her at all, but most of all I wanted to get some sense of what it felt like to be her; and she knew this, and tried to stop too much of that gleaming through the cracks and fissures of her discourse. One thing she said, though: 'I think you like to be in love, Charlie, for all the bad times you've had with it. I don't want this any more. In love I was like a dog, and I was treated like a dog. Now I just use men.' She said this very gaily too, but it sounded to me like a good resolution for New Year, or something she was trying on for size, not a declaration of principle. That was how it felt to me, anyway. It felt like that to me then. I had tunnel vision, of course. To put it mildly. I was like a fucking runaway tube train. And she could have me any way she liked.

We drank another bottle and ate some Polish sausage. She made a big deal out of the Polish sausage, like a kid on a birthday treat, and I realized that it was still a treat for her; it still felt like a treat after so many years in England, to call for it and get it so easily and quickly, as much of it as you wanted; and I imagined her, sixteen years old, even thinner, with her damp black hair plastered over her forehead, queuing for hours in the rain, in a soot-blackened street, in the dirtiest town in Europe, for Polish sausage that might or might not be there when she got to the head of the queue.

When we had finished the Polish sausage (when she had finished hers and half of mine) she wiped her mouth and looked at me for a little while as if she was making her mind up about something. Then she said, 'Would you like to come back and see my place? Have a cup of coffee?'

'Yes, I would,' I said fervently. 'Very much indeed.'

She frowned. 'Listen,' she said. 'Whatever you're thinking, it isn't going to be like you think.'

'I know,' I said. 'I knew it wouldn't be. That's all right. After all, it never bloody well is like I think; that's what makes life so fascinating.'

'Then why do you think it will be like whatever it is, when you know it won't be like that at all?'

'Because I can't bloody well help it.'

This made her laugh. 'OK. Let's go. Off like a foreskin!'

I winced a bit at that, and made a mental note that when I knew her better I would try to get her not to use that particular phrase.

*   *   *

49

I had brought the car that night, because even though I knew it would not be like I thought, and so on . . . It is a Jaguar, my car, and I am very fond of it. (Anything to say about that?) I like it because it is oldish, and quiet, and heavy, and fast, and because it still smells of leather inside despite the thousands of cigarettes that have been smoked in it. I like everything about it except that it is so fond of petrol it wants filling up before it will even go as far as the bloody paper shop. I still like just to look at it out of the window as it crouches down there in the side street under the street lamp. I am looking at it now, in fact, crouched under the street lamp with nowhere to go.

I opened her door first and held it open for her while she got in. This is something else I like to do, and it irritates some women. Muriel, for example, says that she is perfectly capable of opening a car door and getting in under her own steam, thanks very much, and I only do it because I enjoy the role of benign phallocratic despot, which may well be the case for all I know. Viola didn't seem to mind. She even smiled and said thank you, which touched me, because nobody much had been treating me like that recently.

When I had got in myself, I turned and looked at her, and was surprised by the first authentic jolt of desire I'd had since first seeing her. It's like that with me, nearly always. I need to look, and know there's something, then wait, then get closer, understand a little, guess a little, then look again . . . I don't need to touch. I wonder what it's like for you. I don't think I've discussed this before with anyone. You see, I knew it would take time, letting her move about quietly in the darkness behind the bar, letting the tune of her voice

50

roam about my head, letting it all happen, the Polish sausage and all, then looking again.

She looked frail and strong and shy. She was leaning back against the headrest, exposing her throat, and her dress had ridden up above her knees; she looked back at me as if she trusted me, and I felt my prick thickening for her. Such a warm, strong, affectionate sensation after all that frantic narration and unease. I had not touched her once, but I did now. I put my hand over hers and she gripped it tight, not looking at me, and then let it go. Oh, yes. The old quack-quack, as Saul Bellow (I think) encapsulates it.

It is worth it, for moments like these. It is all worth it. I think it is.

I started the engine and she told me where to go. 'Look,' she said, 'I think I better tell you I share this place, where I live. I mean, probably we won't be alone. You'll see this guy, walking about, carrying bits of wood about. Always he's carrying bits of wood about. You can cope with this?'

'Yes, I should think so,' I said.

'Always he's putting up shelves.'

'He's . . . a friend of yours?'

She thought about it. 'No, he's not my friend.'

'It's just a kind of convenience thing? Sharing the rent, or the mortgage?'

'Yes, I suppose. In a way.'

'He's, um . . . an acquaintance?'

She laughed. 'These English words; so strange, some of them. Yes, he's my acquaintance. Anyway, I thought I'd better tell you so you wouldn't be frightened of him.'

'I don't frighten very easily,' I said, which was true. 'Does he frighten people?'

'He's a bit strange sometimes. But he will be all right. We'll drink coffee and talk, and he'll walk about with bits of wood, OK?'

'OK,' I said. It was, really. Anything was OK.

The house, when we got there, was in a scruffy, narrow little Victorian terrace on the far side of the canal, which was more or less what I had expected. Students, Sikhs, and the pale armies of the dispossessed. Possessions, evictions, private violence, domestic violence, unfathomable Asian violence, modest drug dealing, unambitious and clumsily executed burglary, theft and fraud. Ruth's clients' territory. The house outside which we stopped was only three doors away from the house of a client whom I had the previous week successfully shepherded through a guilty plea to receiving five stolen gas cookers, my friend Jim Blatt for the prosecution having failed to establish to the satisfaction of the magistrates that my client had not received them but had stolen them in person – together with fourteen refrigerators, six microwave ovens and an Amstrad word processor with a faulty printer. I had learnt about the faulty printer only after the court case, celebrating our excellent result with my client, when instead of showering me with gratitude and praise for my forensic skills, he had got seriously ratted and bored the tits off me about how he was fucked if he could get the fucker to work and how about that for fucking Taiwan workmanship; he had a good mind to go up the High Street and toss the fucker back through Dixon's fucking plate glass window and see what the fuck the fuckers had to say about that. I told him that I could certainly see his fucking point, and that I looked forward to representing him again as soon as he had carried out his protest. He told me that I could fucking count on that and it was a fucking firm date, and we parted on good terms.

It was that sort of territory: a sort of territory I was coming to feel increasingly comfortable in. I was getting weary of the clients who bought nursing homes and jumped over things on big horses and instructed me to go for other people's jugulars; and beginning to prefer the clients who sat in their vests and stared vaguely out of the window towards distant factory chimneys, and who risked years of their liberty stealing things that didn't even fucking work.

Inside the house was quite different from what one might have expected; but I had expected that too. All the walls and ceilings had recently been painted white, and all the woodwork had recently been painted black, and all the floors had been sanded. What I had not expected was what was on the walls: several hundred large black and white photographic prints, most but not all of them depicting my new Polish friend.

'Christ,' I said, stopping still in the hall.

'Yes, I know; terrible, eh?' she said, and went ahead of me into what I supposed must be the kitchen.

I stayed in the hall and looked at the photographs, which were tacked up four deep on all the walls, and on up the stairs to the landing, where there were more of them. There she was, over and over again, from the front, from the back, from the side, from above, from below, still, on the move, in focus, out of focus, smiling, fierce, blank-faced, dressed, half-dressed, naked. None of them could be described as pornographic, but they had the coldness of pornography. I remembered something I had read somewhere about how primitive peoples believed being photographed stole your soul or something, put you in the power of the photographer; and something Muriel had been trying to convince me of, that in all visual art we are forced to gaze with a cold, male, proprietorial gaze upon a helpless female image. Both these notions suddenly began to make sense. It was something to do with how many images of Viola there were. She had been posed, fixed, recorded, *done*, over and over again. And I remembered a phrase that had stuck in my mind from the first time I read Henry Miller as a kid on a school trip to Paris, about how he was going to fuck that woman so she would stay fucked. It had seemed a splendid and rather heroic endeavour to me at the time; later futile, pathetic, and simply a mistake. But someone had wanted to photograph Viola so that she would stay photographed.

I went into the kitchen. That was full of photographs of her too. She was brewing the coffee. It was real coffee and it smelt very good and strong. But I was bothered by the photographs. I felt I wanted to take them all down and put them somewhere secret; I didn't want to look at them and I didn't want them to be there . . . I think now that I didn't want the way I saw her to be defined for me. Maybe it was that, I don't know. They bothered me.

'Who took the photographs?' I said. She could see that I was bothered.

'That man. He's a photographer, you know.'

'Yes, I rather thought he might be.'

'You don't like them?'

'I think they're very good,' I said. And then, 'No, I hate them.'

'Listen,' she said, 'it's not any big deal. He's a photographer, he wants to make photographs of someone, I am here, so I let him make his photographs of me. Don't be upset.'

'All right,' I said.

* * *

She could have told me to mind my own business, but she permitted me to be upset. That was nice. The other nice thing was that her imperfect English offered me a solution. We take photographs; in other languages they make photographs. We are the primitive people. This photographer had not taken her; he had simply made images which had to do with the way he saw her. She was offering me that way of seeing it and I was grateful.

Now I think photographs are always taken, and the other languages get it wrong.

And what am I doing here, sitting drinking whisky and smoking cigarettes and telling this story: making or taking?

I should stick to the law, which is at least clear; and my feelings, which may be confused, but are at least my own.

We went into the living room, which was black and white like the hall and kitchen, and full of photographs of Viola, but I did not mind the photographs so much now. There were two things to sit on, a black sofa and a black wooden chair with arms. I sat on the sofa and she sat on the floor on a black woollen rug.

I asked her if I could have a drink as well.
    'Coffee is a drink,' she said, grinning.
    'Not in English,' I said. I was starting to feel more comfortable with her.
    'I think there's some brandy?'
    'Yes, that's a drink,' I said. She went and got a bottle of brandy and a glass, and she sat on the black rug and

watched me drinking coffee and brandy while I watched her face and her arms and her hands as she told me about her sister in Poland who was having an affair with a priest. 'People, problems. You know?'

After a while, I heard footsteps coming down the uncarpeted stairs and turned round to see the man standing in the doorway, with two shelves under his arm, as advertised. He was about the same age as me, a short man in shirtsleeves with hairy muscular forearms and very bright piercing eyes. He stood there in the doorway, staring at me with these bright piercing eyes and two shelves under his arm, not saying anything at all, and yet somehow not looking like a total dickhead, which rather impressed me.

'Hi,' she said. 'This is Charlie Cross, he's a solicitor.'

He nodded to me and I said good evening to him in a way that should have indicated that he should now lurk off to his pit, or go and put up another shelf, go away somewhere else and leave me and his acquaintance to further our relationship.

'We're having coffee,' she said. 'D'you want any?'

'I'll have a drink,' he said. He was English.

'You see?' I said to her.

He got himself a glass and sat down on the wooden chair and started to talk to us.

We had what on another occasion would have been a very interesting conversation. It was conducted on blokeist lines, and the Man with the Shelves controlled it. He interviewed me about my work in some detail, seeming particularly interested in the upmarket and jugular side of it. He seemed to grasp very quickly that I had a good working knowledge of how the town was controlled and carved up; how the councillors related to the property dealers (often the same people, in fact); how a prime patch of agricultural land worth sod all to anyone but a few cows and the local ramblers could be metamorphosed into a high-density but tastefully land-scaped estate for executives; how the clerks controlled the magistrates, and so on. His questions were sharp and to the point, so that I didn't need to repeat anything, and every so often he would summarize his understanding of a point with a brutal clarity that most of the local judiciary would have envied. In fact, if I hadn't been wishing so fervently that the sod was several miles, or at least several rooms away, I would have been having a bloody good time.

He was drinking an impressively large quantity of brandy without showing any signs of its effects at all. I was drinking rather slowly by then, for me. After a while, the bottle moved to a place on the floor by the side of his chair, where it stayed. And Viola sat on the floor between us, saying very little; I could not tell what she was thinking or feeling.

Then he started to talk about his own work. He asked me what I thought of the photographs on the walls and I told him that I admired them but found them oppre-sive. 'Good,' he said. They represented a phase that he had exhausted without solving to his satisfaction; he had set himself the problem of photographing another human being in such a way that both the subject (or object) of his images, and the range of response avail-able to the spectator, would be totally controlled and predictable. This total control was the only thing that interested him. He had been absurdly ambitious in choosing the most difficult subject of all to start with, but he did not resent the waste of time and effort. Now he was exploring the same problem with much more modest material: he was photographing cardboard boxes and lengths of string, sometimes separately, sometimes in combination. This, too, was proving extraordinarily difficult. His control over the subject was more or less complete, but paradoxically the problem of viewer response had become even more acute. Even when he looked at his own prints he found it impossible not to invest them with something that was *not there*; to make meanings, make stories, impute relationships, discover emotions, become invaded by memories . . . it was all extremely difficult.

It struck me that it was absolutely impossible, and I said so. It seemed so obviously impossible that I wondered if he was mad, because he was clearly not stupid. I suddenly thought: now he wants to fuck cardboard boxes so that they stay fucked, and he asked me in a rather sharp tone what I was smiling at.

'Well,' I said, realizing for the first time that I was very tired and slightly drunk, 'surely you must realize that's what is going to happen. It's fucking futile, what you're trying to do, isn't it?'

'Of course it is,' he said irritably. 'That's hardly the point. I was assuming that we were both starting from the position that everything is fucking futile, as you put it.'

There was something else there besides irritation, something nastier, but I didn't know what it was, and I didn't want to know. A glum conviction was beginning to take shape in my mind, despite the tunnel vision, despite the champagne, the brandy, the desire, the intoxication of being so close to her body and her soft, bruise-like mouth: this conversation, which had already gone on until two in the morning, was only going to be terminated by one of the three of us getting up and going out; and, somehow, that one was going to have to be me.

So I got up and said I had to be going. Viola scrambled up. He didn't move, except to reach down to the bottle and pour himself another brandy. I said cheerio to him and he nodded.

'I'll see you to your car,' she said.

It wasn't till I was out in the fresh air that it hit me. 'That man,' I said. 'He's not just a man you share the house with who walks around putting up shelves, is he? He's not just your acquaintance, is he?'

She didn't say anything.

'I mean, when I go, you're going to go back in the house, and then you're going to go to bed with him. Aren't you?'

She sighed. 'Oh, yes. I suppose.'

'I am such a fucking fool.'

'I'm so sorry,' she said. 'People, problems, you know?'

We had reached the car. I wished it was something I could pull over my head. I had no business being upset, but I was upset. I hadn't been upset for years and I had forgotten what it felt like. I leant against the car. 'Well,' I said.

Suddenly she had both arms round my neck and her body and face were pressed against mine, her wide mouth open over my mouth, her cool tongue on mine, and almost before I had started to realize what was happening and join in, she had pulled away.

'Listen,' she said, 'we'll arrange things better next time. Promise, OK?' Then she turned and ran into the house.

SIX

SOME YEARS AGO, in the days when I still had Laura
and Joe and Sal, I also had a sweet Alsatian bitch called
Anita. Anita had been brought to us by a friend of ours
called Polly, who went in for rescuing unwanted animals. She had knocked on our door with this terrified,
emaciated, two-year-old Alsatian bitch with a horribly
mangled back leg and no name, who was going to be
put down that day because the tinkers who owned her
and had accidentally run her over on the previous day
were not able, or not willing, to pay the vet's bill. I had
always been frightened of Alsatians but it was hard to
be frightened of this one. She stood on our doorstep,
quivering, trailing her mangled leg, and waited for us
to hurt her some more. And without consulting my
wife and children I said that we would have her and
see how it went.

It was very difficult. The leg was no problem; all it
needed was money and time. The hard thing was
teaching her not to be terrified. She was frightened of
us. She was frightened of other people. She was frightened of other animals. She was frightened of houses,
and especially frightened of carpets and furniture,
though after a few days she felt comparatively safe
cowering under the kitchen table. She was too timid to
bark, too timid even to whine, though I am sure that
she didn't sleep at all for the first few nights: too
frightened to. She had never been for a walk, and when

her leg was strong enough we had to teach her that walks were things to be enjoyed, which was not easy, because she was frightened of grass, trees, and the smells of other dogs. We could detect no personality at all in her except the fear that permeated every cell in her body. She didn't even smile like Charlie Chaplin. Her lovely ears hung off her head like bits of old plasticine. I could not bear to imagine what it must be like to feel the way that she did, not just now and then, but all the time.

But very slowly, over months rather than weeks, we taught her to trust us not to hurt her. She learnt to sleep deeply, though she had bad dreams for a long time. She learnt to eat her share, and stick up for herself with the cats. She got the hang of walks and began to be able to meet other dogs and even enjoy their company. She even got her ears up now and then, which made her look a totally different person. She discovered a startling talent for catching rabbits on the run, turning and twisting after them as they turned and twisted, as if in the grip of some ferocious dream. She would break their backs with a single bite and then stand there with her mouth open and her tongue lolling out, looking totally baffled. Eventually she learnt to fool about and be mildly disobedient, which we were reluctant to check, because for her it was such a triumph over fear.

Most importantly, she learnt to love us. In love she was like a dog, though we treated her like a person. She never used us, though I suppose we used her, to express the love it was difficult to feel for each other. We were better with her than we were with each other. We liked each other better for the way we were with her. She taught us to be better people than we could have been without her. Dogs are better people than people are. She is dead now, of course.

When I moved out she stayed with Laura, and when I went to see them it was more painful to see her than it was to see Laura. I would take her out on my own, as other men take their children to the zoo or the park, and when I got back to the flat I would take her for walks in my mind, and sometimes when I slept I would take her for walks in my dreams.

The time I hate to remember, I had taken her to Brownhill Wood. Brownhill Wood was her favourite place. It was hilly, and thick with birch trees and brambles. The soil there was unusually thin and sandy, and had eroded into dramatic, quarry-like indentations and precipitous slopes. It was studded with rabbit warrens and several foxholes. Anita was always beside herself with excitement when she went there, hurling herself recklessly down the steep embankments, crashing into the brambles, disappearing entirely for minutes while I yelled for her, then reappearing with her foolish grin on the path in front of me as if she had materialized out of thin air.

We were walking along the top path, near the grounds of the convent. Just below the top path was one of the foxholes. I heard scrabbling behind me and turned to see Anita half in and half out of the foxhole. It looked as if she had gone in head first, then tried to turn, and in doing that dragged a lot of loose sandy earth in after her. She had got her head free so that she could breathe, but she couldn't get herself out.

As I went to help her, I felt the earth slip and crumble under my feet. Some of it went into the foxhole, burying her up to the neck; most of it stayed where it was, burying me up to the knees. I knew that I was in no danger of being buried completely, but I would lose Anita within a matter of minutes unless I could do something to help her. She was looking towards me, panting but not whimpering, distressed but not panicking, utterly confident that I was going to save her. The trouble was that I could not get my feet out of the sand to get really close to her. By reaching forward as far as I could, I managed to get my hands round her collar, and I pulled. My movement dislodged some more loose earth and some of it went into her mouth and her eyes. I pulled harder. Something gave. But something was terribly wrong. Something had her down there, by the back legs, and I realized that if I pulled with all my strength, I would pull her apart. I was weeping and whimpering by now. All I could think of to do was to hold on to her collar with just enough strength to stop her from being sucked down into the hole away from me. That was the best I could do for her. She stared into my face, panting. Her eyes never left mine. She was utterly confident that I was going to save her.

It's three in the morning. There are twenty-seven dog-ends in the ashtray. There is half an inch of Bell's left in the bottle. Down in the street my car crouches under the street lamp. I have been crying again, but now I have stopped. In seven hours I am going into action on behalf of a legless client of mine. His wife, who has left him, is suing him for divorce and maintenance on the grounds of mental cruelty. She says that he forced her to have sex with other women in front of him because he got off on it. She has made up this story because she wants to get half of a) his flat and b) his disability pension. He still loves her and wants her back. There is always someone worse off than you, as my father used to say.

* * *

What do you think about people? D'you think it's been a success on the whole? Don't you think it's time they came up with a better idea?

I would like to describe her properly, but it is difficult because there were so many of her, and when I think about her she is nearly always in motion. Tall, thin, black hair, wide mouth. Sullen, my first impression. That was a mistake, to do with her mouth. Her lips were so wide and full that they sometimes seemed swollen, bruised . . . and she didn't feel she had to be doing something with her mouth the whole time, like most people; the way they feel they have to look determined or alert, or pleasant . . . when she was daydreaming, or just listening, or lying about doing nothing, she would just let it alone to be a mouth, if you see what I mean. When she did do something with it, it usually happened very quickly indeed. Her toothy, little-girl smile, her doorstep pout, her cynical grin, came and went so quickly that I wanted action replays in slow motion. Her nose, let us face it, was a bit of a blob, but I would not have had it any other way, and always refused to lend her the money for the nose job she kept threatening to have. I could lie for hours, just browsing quietly on her nose. Irish blow jobs, we called them. (All right. Sometimes I do make Irish jokes.) Her eyes were dark green and sometimes dark brown and sometimes black. I am unable to explain this. She was absurdly proud of her ears, which were indeed small and very elegantly shaped, their lobes so delicate and soft and translucent they seemed too intimate to be exposed in public . . .

No, it's no good. I must be boring you, and I'm not getting anywhere near, not really. If you could see the photographs, the real ones, and the ones that start flashing up on the backs of my eyelids whenever I close

64

my eyes . . . there she is, over and over again; from the front, from the back, from the side, from above, from below, still, on the move, in focus, out of focus, smiling, fierce, blank-faced, laughing, crying, coming, dressed, half-dressed, naked. Still not enough, still not her.

I suppose I see this as a story of destructive passion, but I would be as mad as he was if I tried to control your response. You might see it as a light comedy, or a last wheezy gasp from the ruins of the crumbled phal-locentric edifice, or a banal case history, or an unreliable guide to middle-class mores in the late eighties, of particular interest to those researching the workings of the English legal system. Feel free. Make your own meanings.

After the night of the photographer, I went about my work feeling bothered, churned and excited. It was the first time since Laura, you see, that I had felt that possibility. I had, of course, made one or two attempts to get myself going again in the sexual arena. They reminded me of those groups I was on about the other night. One of the things they had you doing, these groups, was thumping cushions to get in touch with your anger. The idea was that if you thumped hard enough and long enough and yelled loud enough, you would start to feel a glimmer of the real thing; and then, before you knew what was happening to you, you'd be snarling and growling and going purple in the face, and hurling yourself all over the room and smash-ing things, and everybody would be very pleased with you and thank you for sharing your anger with them. The odd thing was that it worked. Rather alarming, in a way. I think the theory was that the more anger you had repressed in your life, the more violent the outburst would be when you finally got in touch with it. So that the most extreme manifestations would emanate from timid women who had always leaked tears instead of blowing their tops. In fact, the real performers were more often blokes like me, who, one would have thought, had reasonably convenient access to their anger in everyday life. The more you expend, the more you have to give, in this as in other spheres of the emotional life. This is just anecdotal evidence, you understand. I dare say they've done studies at the Open University. I found it, as I say, a bit alarming.

And what was Charlie Cross, your reliable, local, legal beagle, doing at one of these, well, hippyish gatherings? Well (he confessed) I had heard about them from one of my clients, who had given me the impression that there was a certain amount of mindless fucking to be had at them, and that was something I felt I needed and deserved at the time. She was quite right about that aspect of it. But what I found when I got there was that what I really wanted to do was cry a lot and work on my problem, which was acute sexual jealousy (in relation to Laura), and somehow move from rage and despair to bargaining and acceptance, which I succeeded in doing, in her case, and thought I was free of it for ever. Wrong. Wrong, wrong, wrong.

The point about the cushion-thumping was that that was what it seemed like, trying to get going with other women. Going through the motions as if I meant it, hoping that I would start to get a glimmer of the real thing. There was an extremely nice-looking secretary at the county court who had always rather liked the look of me, and I thumped the cushion hard and long with her for a week or two; only metaphorically, you understand. In fact I was extraordinarily gentle and considerate and gentlemanly with her, which was part of the problem, because that was all I felt like being with her. We could *do* it all right, but it always seemed such an odd thing to be doing. I think she felt the same way too. I sometimes caught this look on her face when she thought I wasn't looking at her, as if she was thinking, well, this ought to be fine, and in a sense it is fine, so why does it feel like evening classes?

And then there was Ruth. Oh dear. We were such good friends that we could hardly get it on at all. We'd keep stopping in the middle to discuss interesting clients and points of law, and the extraordinary interpretations Ruth's analyst had been making lately, to the extent that we often forgot to finish what we were supposed to be doing. The coital position we always seemed to get into was lying on our sides, face to face, propping our heads on our elbows, rather like a couple of participants in Plato's *Symposium*. Exactly like that, I dare say, now I come to think about it. It was very good for our friendship and very bad for everything else, and it made me very depressed. Eventually I had to tell her that it wasn't working and we should go back to being friends. She said she was relieved I'd said it first, because she too had felt something was lacking; but in fact I think she was rather upset about it, and that was partly why she left the firm and bequeathed me all her ratty, desperate clients. From some things she had said, I guessed that this was how it had often been for her. That's what you get for going to bed with people you like. It's *all right* to like the person, of course – in fact it makes it sweeter in a way – but the essential thing, I am afraid, is that it has to be someone who can do you harm.

Well that was all very pleasant and gentle and avuncular and boring old fartish, wasn't it? I was meaning to tell you about that cat I couldn't get off my face without strangling it. Not in the vein, it seems. Perhaps I'm starting to get better.

I left it a few days before going back to Guido's because I wanted to get some control over the bother and the churning and the excitement. I did some gentle convey-ancing and allowed myself one heady treat: getting a case thrown out against a not very bright client of mine who was accused of setting fire to a cricket pavilion. Did you know that you can get ten years for arson? My client was fond of a bit of a blaze, as many of us are, and had not been able to give the police a convincing reason for being first on the scene. The fire was, in fact, I was reliably informed, the work of the club secretary who had the full backing of the selection committee, and a very efficient job it was too. But after failing to nail my client, the police rather lost heart over the whole affair; and now, what with the insurance money and the public appeal, the club has a very smart new pavilion which was formally opened the other week by the lord lieutenant of the county, a well-known local shitbag. I was at the ceremony myself and got mildly ratted at the bar. As is my wont.

She was there again. It felt as bad as ever. I sat down at the table and waited for her to come over. She walked across with her quick bouncy walk, smiled at me and then looked down. She's as nervous as I am, I thought.

'Hello,' she said, 'do you want a bottle of champagne?'

'Just a large Scotch, please,' I said.

'What's the matter, are you angry with me? Don't you like me any more?'

'I've been thinking about you all week.'

She smiled again. 'So have I. So why didn't you come before?'

'I was trying to be cool about it.'

'Ha!' she said. 'That's no good.'

'I know,' I said. 'Well, I'm here now.'

'OK, I'll get your whisky.' She strode off to the bar.

I looked round. The Sikh hit men were in again. One of them raised a hand to me and I nodded.

She came back with the whisky. 'Listen, you know this is all a big mistake I think.'

'I don't think so,' I said.

She bit her lip and looked at me for a moment or two. 'Well. He's going away Friday. To London. Staying the night. You can come round and see me if you like.'

'Yes, I'd like that very much,' I said.

'Can you come about eight?'

'Yes.'

'Good. This is all a big mistake, you know.'

'No, it isn't.'

She smiled. 'I'm very happy you're coming,' she said. 'The office is closed now.'

And she went off behind the bar. She didn't come near me again that evening. The guy with the moustache that everyone called Guido, although he was Polish, brought me two more big ones at half-hour intervals, and I sat and drank them and watched her moving about quietly behind the bar, though it was too dark to see the expression on her face.

A man owns a cat, of which he is very fond, but the cat has gone mad. It springs at the man's face and claws at his cheeks and his eyes. He grabs the cat and holds it away from him, and the cat lunges at him with its powerful back legs, its claws ripping at the inside of his forearm. He flings the cat down and it leaps at his face again. He is streaming with blood now. He realizes that the only way to subdue the cat is to strangle it. He squeezes the cat's throat as the cat's claws tear at his arms, ripping the skin into ribbons. All he can do is keep squeezing. Eventually the cat's struggles get weaker and it starts to die. But he doesn't want to kill the cat because he is fond of it. He relaxes his grip and lets it slide to the floor. Almost immediately it revives and springs at his face again. He holds it away from him and starts to strangle it, as its claws scrabble down the bloody flesh of his forearms. All he can do is to keep squeezing. It goes on like this for a long time and it hurts very much indeed.

SEVEN

SOMEONE HAD TAKEN down all the photographs of
Viola. There were new photographs on the walls. They
were of empty cardboard boxes and pieces of string,
mostly separately, some in combination. I stood in the
doorway feeling huge and clumsy and spare in my big
suit, dangling a bottle of champagne and a bottle of
Scotch like a couple of Indian clubs. She stood there
looking at me, and I thought how irresolute we both
were. She was wearing the same black dress, but no earrings this time. She looked very clean and her hair was
damp. I was very clean too. I had showered and shaved
myself mercilessly and washed my hair and doused
myself in Chanel for Blokes and cut my fingernails and
toenails. We were both so clean under our clothes.

She stepped towards me, her hands down by her
side, until we were touching, and started to kiss my
face with soft, little-girl kisses. Her body felt damp and
cool but her lips were very warm and soft; she smelt of
soap and shampoo, but also increasingly and unmistakeably of herself, and I felt my dick quicken to her
and started to feel warm and safe. I wanted to put my
Indian clubs down and hold her to me, and she sensed
this, and pulled away, and took my hand and dragged
me into the living room, smiling.

'I have to tell you I am very nervous,' she said. 'I had
a little puke about an hour ago.'

'I'm nervous too,' I said.

'Good,' she said. 'Let's have a drink.'

* * *

71

I am not a man who sits on floors. I sat on the black sofa and she kicked her flat black shoes off and sat on the floor at my feet, and we drank some of the champagne. She talked a little about the Man with the Shelves: how she had tried to love him but he wouldn't let himself be loved; about how he couldn't bear her but couldn't let her go; how he couldn't get to sleep unless he had his arm tight around her like a vice so she lay all night like a rabbit in a trap; how they used each other. After not very much of this I could feel my genitalia quaking and shrivelling as if they wanted to squeeze back inside me and hide and I said that if she didn't mind, I'd rather we didn't talk about the Man with the Shelves any more.

'I'm sorry,' she said. 'Just one more thing. The other night, when I went back in the house, as soon as I came into the room, he says: that guy, you're having an affair with him, aren't you? I said, no, of course I'm not, I've just talked to him a couple of times in Guido's. He was giving me terrible hardeye you know, it was like third degree. And then he said: well, whether you're having an affair with him or not, he's having an affair with you. I go: oh, yes, and how do you make that out? He says: body language, you bitch. He thinks he can read body language, you know.' She grinned and scrambled up on the sofa, leaned back against the arm, facing me, and put her bare feet in my lap like a present. 'I think maybe what he can read is the future, yes?' she said.

I took her long pale feet in my hands; they felt cool, and still slightly damp, and I warmed them for her, remembering a time when Sal, aged two, had wrapped one of her fat little feet in Christmas paper and given it to me as a present. Viola curled her toes round my fingers. She had long and clever toes and I tried not to think about whose fingers she had curled them round before. She was with me now. After a while, she wiggled them in my lap, in a gentle, exploratory way. Neither of us looked down. We looked into each other's eyes. She was smiling slightly and I was smiling increasingly broadly, probably grinning like an idiot, as her blind, clever toes fumbled and found their way.

'Listen,' she said, 'this is going to be all right, in a strange way, even if it isn't; you know what I mean?'

'Yes,' I said. I felt very grateful to her for saying that, because it is so rarely all right the first time, though very occasionally, even when it isn't, it is. In a strange way.

'OK,' she said, taking my hand. 'Let's go.'

She led me upstairs to a bedroom I didn't see, except that it had a bed in it and it had her in it. She lit two candles, turned to face me, smiling shyly, and pulled her dress over her head. She had nothing on underneath except a pair of skimpy black pants, and she slipped them off too – she was as quick as a fish – and stood resting her thin body lightly against me, her face against my chest. I could feel her warm breath through my shirt, and I felt huge and clumsy and encumbered, and wondered how she could possibly want this. It's so hard for us to understand what women want in men, when they want us, so easy to believe them when they don't.

She got into bed but she didn't pull the sheet over her. She lay propped up on her elbows smiling at me. 'So you're going to take your things off, or not?'

She looked at me all the time I was undressing, which seemed to take for ever, but it was my face she was looking at, not my body, which made things a little better. The candles threw big shadows. Her face was in shadow but her eyes were bright. I got in beside her and heard the springs creak: I weigh over thirteen stone. She looked so fragile. I had this irrational fear that I might break her in some way. She touched my shoulder lightly, and kissed me lightly on the lips, then

73

took my cock on her hand and bent over it, as if in a biology lesson.

'You're not circumcised! You didn't tell me this!' She seemed astonished, though not displeased.

'Er . . . should I have?' I said.

'But of course. It's so surprising. I haven't seen one like this since I was thirteen, in Poland. It's very pretty, you know.' Together we watched the embarrassed sceptre of my manhood wilting under our scrutiny. 'I'm sorry,' she said. 'I think this is not very considerate of me. Come on. Lie down. Lie down quietly by me.'

I did what she told me, and felt the thin length of her against me, her breath against my face, and ran my fingers down the sweet knobbly road of her spine, and held one cheek of her tight muscular bum in my hand. Very lightly, so that she would feel free to move, remembering what she had said about the Man with the Shelves. We kissed so softly that our mouths seemed to have no shape, so long that we seemed to have one face between the two of us. I felt myself thickening and stiffening again, and felt her feel that too, and I was so sure that she would slither on top of me that I was surprised when she pulled my weight on top of her. My face was far enough away from hers to be able to see her properly now. She was smiling. She was smiling as if she trusted me not to hurt her, or as if she understood that I would hurt her but she trusted me just the same . . . no, that's not quite it, that's not all of it; it was a brave smile, but it was friendly, too, as if this was something that might hurt us both, but something we could get through together. Her thighs were wide apart, defenceless, and she moved delicately under me, finding a conjunction that was pleasing for both of us, and after a while I could see her eyes go vague and misty and she started to sigh. I reached down, but she stopped me. 'No. Let him find his own way.'

* * *

74

It was a good trick she had there, and again I found myself trying not to think about where she had learnt it and how long it had taken her to perfect it, as her blind, clever sex reached for mine, circled round it and showed it where to go, while her wide intelligent eyes looked into my eyes. The eagle sees everything, except where the mole sees. She was wonderfully warm and wet and slippery, but narrow, and her eyes went very wide as I went into her. She was still smiling, though. I was up on my elbows, keeping my weight off her; I didn't want to crush her or stop her moving, and I thought it was so nice that she was smiling, as if she was telling me that this terrible thing that we were doing was all right and something that had to be done, and nothing that either of us should blame each other for. Her arms were up above her head, but very relaxed, and her small breasts had almost disappeared as breasts. Delicate pinky-fawn nipples that I bent and licked lightly: and she laughed and moved under me to take the whole length of me, and growled deep in her throat, and then laughed again at the sound of her growling; and suddenly it seemed like not a terrible thing at all, but something very relaxed and pleasant that we were sharing, like a witty conversation with no pressure to sparkle, but in which we were somehow quite effortlessly finding things to say to each other that were subtle and relevant and friendly and pleasing, and I thought: this actually is actually all right, not just all right even though it isn't, and I felt long and strong in her and lordly and safe, and as if I could go slowly on like this for ever; and I held still for what seemed like whole long minutes, while she moved around me and under me, pleasing herself and pleasing me, and smiling, smiling all the time; and I found myself smiling too; and then she laughed, and I thought she must be laughing at the daft grin I probably had all over my face; and I said, 'What?'

'Nothing,' she said. 'It's just so nice, this, you know?

I didn't think you would be so gentle, I thought you would be a wham bang man.'

'I am, sometimes,' I said.

'Good,' she said.

She stretched out one of her long legs and dangled it gaily and nonchalantly over my shoulder, stroking the nape of my neck with her toes.

'Goodness me,' I said.

'What?'

'You're tremendously supple, aren't you?'

She put her hands behind her head and grinned up at me. 'Aren't we all?' She lifted her other leg and folded it companionably round my back, moving it gently up and down, while I wondered in a blurred sort of way what she had meant, and where I had heard that phrase before, in some recent but quite foreign context; something was moving, dark and blurred, in the shadows at the back of my mind . . .

'Come on,' she said. 'Concentrate.' And she pulled me down on top of her, sighing as my weight pressed her down into the bed, and stretched her arms straight up over her head, and opened her mouth wide under mine, and tilted her hips up to take even more of me, and I realized almost immediately that I had been quite wrong about being able to go on like that for ever, and that I didn't in the least want to.

'Yes,' she said. 'Come on. Come on. Come. Come in me.'

And I felt that she wanted me to drive hard into her, thud against her, jolt her into orgasm; but I couldn't, didn't want to; what was happening to me felt so strange, as if I wanted to lose myself in her, dissolve in her, and I came almost motionless inside her, except that I was trembling all over, down to my toes, and weeping too, without sobs, the way women weep, women for whom weeping is easy; and I wanted to tell her how strange it felt, but my mouth was too soft and shapeless to form the message I couldn't find the words

76

for, and she pulled my head down into her neck and
held me until I had stopped trembling and weeping.

'Good,' she said, softly.

And I felt and thought absolutely nothing except
good.

I wonder if everyone wants to die like that.

After a while, a few vague thoughts flopped lazily into
my head: that she had not come, and that perhaps we
should do something about that; that I was crushing
her lovely clever body, and perhaps we should do
something about that too. I shifted a bit, but she
whispered, 'No, don't leave me, not yet. Let's have a
little sleep, like this.' She made a couple of small careful
adjustments, so that I was still in her, though only half
on her, yawned, and snuggled her face into my neck;
and I drifted almost immediately into a dream in which
I was walking round the back streets very late at night
and then climbing the stairs to a club that was and
wasn't Guido's, where I had to hold a case conference
with Mike Gibson and a Sikh called Dhillon; and I was
walking towards the table in the darkest corner of the
bar, and Dhillon raised his hand to me not to come over
just yet, and this was something to do with the third
person at the table, who was a smallish, pale man in
his thirties, dressed only in a white vest and pants . . .
there was something wrong with this man; he seemed
to be dying, and they wanted me to wait until he had
finished dying before I joined them. I walked over to
the dark bar to get myself a drink, but there was no one
to serve me, and somewhere close by someone was
crying softly, and I thought it was Viola.

And I half woke and remembered where I was, in bed
with Viola, her arm round my neck and her face against

my shoulder; but she was trembling and whimpering, and I put my arm round her and explained to her that it was all right, we were just having a bad dream, but everything was all right, she was safe and I was looking after her, and she started to laugh, and I woke up properly and looked into her laughing face.

'What?' I said. 'I thought you were crying, I thought you were having a bad dream.'

'I was just trying to have a little wank, matter of fact,' she said.

I thought, no one's ever said anything like that to me before.

'This is all right?' she said.

'Yes, of course. Um . . . feel free.'

'I'm a bit shy about this.'

'Don't be. Please.'

I kissed her and put my hand over hers, between her legs, and she smiled shyly and began to move gently against me, looking into my eyes and smiling the whole time she was caressing herself until she gasped and pressed her wide open mouth against my neck and shuddered and whimpered, her whole body shaking against mine; and I thought, no one's ever trusted me quite like that before.

She slept for half an hour, and I watched till she woke. It was lovely watching her sleep and it was lovely watching her wake.

'Oh, it's you,' she said, smiling. 'Hey, listen. You hungry?'

'Yes, I am.'

'So am I. Small snag here; I don't cook.'

'You can't cook?'

'I won't cook.'

We put some clothes on and walked through a small scrubby public garden towards the lights of a little row

78

of takeaways: chip shop, Chinese, Indian and Greek. We chose the Greek and sat hand in hand watching the television, on which a man called Harry Enfield was impersonating a Greek takeaway owner called Stavros. Viola started to laugh and I was embarrassed for the guy serving us, who had a fine black moustache and looked not unlike the comedian on the screen, until he turned the heat down over our sizzling lamb and started laughing at the screen himself.

'He's a clever bugger, that one,' he said in a thick local accent. 'Well, we all have to come from some-where, don't we like?'

'I am from Poland,' said Viola.

'Are you duck? That don't surprise me in the least.'

'But I am not a duck, I am a woman.'

'No offence,' he said. He was looking at me to see how he should take it. I could see how she liked to disconcert people, and wondered why she should choose to be so nice to me.

A wind had got up while we were in the Greek place and as we walked back through the scrubby little park it pulled at the trees and sent scraps of rubbish and old newspapers whirling round our legs. She clung to my arm and started to laugh again.

'What?'

'Would you still love me if I was a duck?'

Back in the house I drank some Scotch and smoked a couple of cigarettes and Viola sat on the floor and told me about some of her other sisters. Then we went back to bed to do some more sleeping.

'Turn round,' she said, and I turned away from her, and felt her fit herself into the shape my back made, her knees warm against the backs of my knees. Drifting into sleep, I remembered what she had said as she clung to my arm while the rubbish whirled about us and thought with a pang of unease: she thinks I'm in love with her; she's so simple, she thinks this means that. And then the unease went as I moved into dreams with the sweet stupid thought; she is right, I am.

Some time later, I woke. She was sleeping very still beside me, face down, and she had thrown her pillow off the bed. I stroked her bony back very lightly, feeling the downy hair under my fingers, and she stirred a little but didn't wake; such a sweet bit of her, that downy curve between the small of her back and her tail. I let the weight of my hand rest heavily on it, and she pushed gently up against my hand like a cat teaching me how to stroke her, still breathing the heavy regular breathing of deep sleep; and after a while I let my hand slide down between her cheeks, my fingers tangled in her hair, holding her in the palm of my hand, and she gave a little contented grunt, squeezing my hand between her thighs, holding it closer, her cunt still wet and warm and open, my fingers now half buried in her; she sighed, and opened herself to get more of me, and as I moved on top of her she lifted her hips to let my penis slide into her, moaning and starting to come almost before I was all the way in, her strong buttocks straining up against my belly, her legs trembling; and I found myself opening my mouth very wide and taking the nape of her neck between my teeth, and holding her like that as I started to come inside her, thinking, cats, we're like two cats, this is how cats fuck, and then nothing, as the come seemed to go on and on; and then it was over, and I lay on her in the dark, hearing our harsh, fast breathing gradually soften and slow down, as I licked the salty sweat from her shoulders.

'Blimey,' she said indistinctly and drifted into sleep again.

* * *

It was light outside when I woke again and found that we were lying side by side; she kissed me, smiling, kissed my mouth and my nose and my cheeks and my eyelids, then wriggled down slowly, tracing a path with her pointed tongue over my chin and down my throat and chest, over my belly towards my sleeping cock. She took me in her mouth and held me there gently, as I held her face between my hands, stroking her eyelids with my thumbs, my little fingers in her ears, still half asleep, but lengthening and strengthening and thickening; and she came up, laughing, and pulled me into her again, and I thrust into her hard and fast, without finesse, my mind a blur, and our faces so close that hers was a blur beneath me, her eyes wide and black, her mouth open and gasping: it was like a desperate race, or some kind of struggle in which we were fighting, but both on the same side; I think I was shouting, and she started to cry out, her contractions so strong that for a moment I imagined she was going to take me off at the root, and she pulled her head sharply away and stared at me with a face that seemed angry and astonished, mouth wide open, cheeks dark, eyes black, and grabbed my hair and forced my head back as I exploded into her (I'm sorry but that was actually what it felt like) and fell half across her, gasping, feeling my heart pounding and seeing jerking black shapes like tadpoles dancing behind my eyelids.

Some time later, I was able to ask her if she was all right.

'I don't know,' she said. 'Yes, I think.'

'I was afraid I'd hurt you.'

'No, I don't think I'm hurt.'

'Was it any good, did you like it?'

She lifted herself on to one elbow and looked down at me, her face very serious. 'Did I *like* it? It was like being *raped by a zombie*!'

My face must have showed the consternation I felt,

because she collapsed into laughter; weak, helpless, hysterical laughter, falling across me so that I could feel her belly laughing into mine, and I started to laugh too as she struggled to speak. 'I am thinking – I am thinking, Jesus – I am fucking here with – I am fucking here with one of the living dead!' It was quite a while before either of us could speak properly.

When I could, I said, 'What are we going to do about all this?'

'I don't know,' she said. 'I don't know. This is one terrible situation we are in here, I think.'

We started to laugh again, although it hurt to laugh now, it felt like an illness. I held her hand. I felt as if we had been washed up somewhere, two survivors of some catastrophe. I had seen her for the first time ten days ago, and now I couldn't remember what it felt like not to have her in my head.

A bit later, we went into the bathroom and peed in turn, and then stood together under the shower and washed each other. I soaped her little breasts gently, and raised a magnificent lather on her thick, black, tangled pubic hair. She took the soap from me and stroked it gently along my cock, cradling it in her hands, and in fuddled disbelief I watched it rise again.

'I'm sorry, Charlie,' she said, as she slipped it inside her. 'Not to do anything, just to feel you there; you're not angry?'

I shook my head and leaned back against the tiles, and she leaned on me, her hair black and shiny and plastered close to her small round skull under the streaming water. I believe I dozed off standing up, and I think she did too because she started violently and woke me up again. She turned the shower off and we dried each other with a white towel and a black towel, and walked back to the bedroom, hand in hand.

*   *   *

'Now,' she said very firmly, 'we have to get dressed and be sensible people; there is more to life than laughter and fucking I think.' She pulled on a skimpy black vest that only came down as far as the small of her back, and stood in front of a tall mirror, dragging a comb through her hair, her legs apart, and I wanted her again immediately. I came up behind her and put my arm round her waist, drawing her back against me and slipping my hand under her, and she gave a little hopeless, despairing moan, her face below mine in the mirror, her eyes widening again as I went into her; and we fucked standing up until our knees gave way, then fucked slowly on the floor, patiently, exhaustedly, until I squeezed out one last sweet, aching come, with nothing to come with; I felt as if I had fucked myself into pure, unadulterated spirit, I felt . . . distilled. Dissolved.

Somehow we got ourselves down to the kitchen and made coffee and sat at the kitchen table drinking it, and I managed to light a cigarette although my fingers were still trembling. I don't think we said anything until it was time for me to go, and then, as she opened the door, she said, 'Do you think you will want to see me again?'

I felt a pain in my chest as if she had hit it with a hammer. 'Christ,' I said. 'Of course I want to see you again.'

'Yes,' she said, nodding. 'Me as well. Oh dear; people. Problems.'

I turned to look at her just before I got into the car. She was standing in the doorway, miming a little girl crying. Bottom lip stuck out like a doorstep. Knuckles in her eyes. I got in the car and drove away.

I knew she'd made me happy. But I didn't know how deep she had got into me. Even then; even that soon. Well, I know now.

* * *

Denial. Despair. Denial. Bargaining. Despair. Denial. Bargaining. Denial. Despair.

Acceptance? Don't make me laugh.

I am not stupid: I can talk to myself rationally. I can say, look, you had that, you really had that, how many people ever get near anything like that? They can't take it away from you. If you had it, you still have it. Apart from when you were actually inside her, just a few hundred thousand seconds in a lifetime, it was all memory anyway. Memory and anticipation. I have nothing to anticipate now but bad stuff. Climbing the dark stairs, Dhillon's admonitory hand, waiting for the man in the white underwear to finish dying. Waiting to find out what I am going to do with this yellow dog that smiles at me across the room.

Listen, Charlie, this is not helping. Concentrate. If you had it, you still have it. No. If I haven't got it now, and I haven't, I never had it. Listen: you thought you were one of the living dead but you managed to send out a message to her that she could read. If it happened with her, it could happen with someone else. No. I don't want anyone else. And I cannot believe that this has happened. Charlie, stuff like this happens all the time. Look what happened to the Man with the Shelves. You took that in your stride pretty comfortably, didn't you? Felt a bit sorry for him, naturally; but basically it wasn't your problem, it was his, as they say at the Open University, right? And what about the way he solved his problem? A bit heavy – about as heavy as it goes in point of fact – but he exercised an option that we all have. Right. And very fortunate that you were around, being a man who knows the form in these circumstances. But I couldn't imagine how he felt, then. Now I know. I feel like his brother. Charlie, I am not at all convinced by this. You are not at all like the Man with the Shelves. You have too much curiosity. He was trying to shut everything down. You are going to hang in there, because your bottom line, as the jugular clients say, is that you still want to know what's going to happen.

I have to meet my client at his place of business, a wholesale butchery plant and slaughterhouse. We are walking through this cold cathedral-like hall in our overcoats, discussing the timing of the planning permission application. On either side of us, the huge, pale, frozen carcases dangle from hooks, some motionless, some turning gently in the wind coming through the open door. One of them looks rather strange, and I glance up at it and realize that it's my mother. I decide not to say anything to my client about this, and we walk on, down the cold echoing hall.

EIGHT

THE NEXT NIGHT, I was sitting in my flat staring vaguely at the Harry Holland, running the movie of my night with Viola over and over in my head, trying to absorb it, trying to make it part of me, and even having difficulty in believing elements of it. Wondering what to do about it. Feeling that from the point of view of aesthetic form, as well as the dictates of common sense, the right thing would be to leave it at that. Because in the nature of things, after a start like that, it could only go downhill. So: tell her it was beautiful, and I'd always remember her, but that something like that was by its very nature unique and unrepeatable. Something that neither of us, that nobody, could go on living up to. I quite impressed myself with this line of reasoning, but I also felt that I needed a little time to dwell on it, to be quite sure that it was the right decision. I thought that a week would be enough, and not too hard on her . . . in any case she was probably coming to the same conclusion herself. Yes: I would leave it a week, then go down to Guido's and tell her, and we would both feel very sad and wise about the whole thing. Sad and wise, but blessed, too, in a way. Yes. What a load of crap.

I had a record on the hi-fi while I was thinking all this, Ashkenazy playing Chopin Nocturnes, which lent a sort of spurious grandeur to my musing; in fact it made me feel as if I was possessed by an almost clairvoyant perspicacity. When the record finished, I switched off the hi-fi, put my jacket on, and walked down to Guido's.

She wasn't there.

I drank one large Scotch, went back to the flat and drank three more, then lay on the bed and masturbated ferociously, seeing her over and over; from the front, from the back, from the side, from above, from below, laughing, smiling, blank-faced, motionless, on the move, clothed, half-clothed, naked.

The next night, I managed to wait until ten o'clock before going there again. When I walked into the dark room, the first person I saw was Mike Gibson, sitting at a table by himself, drinking whisky.

'Charlie,' he said. 'This is very unexpected of you. Let's get that nasty girl over and order a bottle of champagne, shall we? Just for badness?'

'All right,' I said.

When she came over, she looked dreadful, as if she had been up all night banging her head against the wall. Dark circles under her eyes, slack mouth, lank hair. She stood listlessly in front of us, not looking at me once, looking at Mike only fleetingly. I wanted very much to pick her up and carry her away and tuck her up warm somewhere and stroke her to sleep.

'Hello,' said Mike. 'Remember us?'

'No,' she said.

'We like a glass of champagne; does that refresh your memory?'

'You want a bottle of champagne?'

'We do, we do, and bring a glass for yourself as well.'

She went off to the bar, came back with the bottle and two glasses and put them on the table.

'You won't join us?'

She didn't say anything.

'Come on, why not? There can't be any harm in it, now can there?'

'Sorry,' she said. 'The office is closed.' She went back behind the bar and we watched her moving about quietly in the darkness.

'She doesn't like us, Charlie,' said Mike.

I thought, you're wrong; she likes me, and she just doesn't want you to know.

He wanted to talk again about the man I thought of as Dog Smile. Dog Smile had been charged by now with three murders, and was remanded in custody in Cardiff. Mike wanted to know whether I could ever imagine myself doing anything like that. I said, no, I couldn't – then.

'D'you ever think,' he said, 'that poor fellows like that, who can't help themselves, that they might be sort of doing these terrible things on behalf of the rest of us? Like, they do it so that we don't have to; does that make any sense at all?'

I said that I didn't want anyone going round murdering women on my behalf.

'No, no, you're right, of course,' he said. 'But it nags at me, Charlie, not being able to understand another human being at all. I mean, most of this weird kind of sexual stuff, if you think about it, we've all got it in us . . . I mean, I'd been through most of the sexual deviations by the time I was seven years old; just playing in the field, tying up, being strangled, being pissed on, f.s., g.s., v.a.; you name it, we all have, am I right now?'

I told him that he was, broadly speaking, not wanting to be having this conversation at all, but at the same time recalling with vivid clarity inspecting the bottom of a fellow infant called Doreen as she extruded a large golden turd in accordance with my instructions, in the patch of waste and mud at the bottom of our garden.

'And when we're very little, before we've started to

88

manufacture the old super-ego, don't we dream of doing terrible, final, obliterating things to people?'

I said I couldn't really remember anything like that.

'Well, it might be just me then,' he said, 'but I doubt that, I really do. Often wonder about being a doctor, of course. Dare say we all do. Surgeons, now, it's well known that a lot of them are sadists who've managed to achieve some level of control and a socially sanctioned outlet. It's a terrible thing to cut a person open and fool about with their insides, you know, Charlie. Mind you, it doesn't do to talk about these things to one's patients.'

'Mike,' I said. 'I *am* a patient.'

'Not one of mine, though, for Christ's sake.' He looked at me sharply. 'Ah, Charlie, I'm sorry, you know I was just thinking aloud, I wouldn't want to bother anyone with my old rag and bone shop.'

'It's OK. Just I've been feeling a bit . . . churned, lately.' And a bit ecstatic, too, I thought, experiencing a sharp desire to tell him about my magic night in the black and white house, and make him understand why I didn't want to think about men doing nasty things to women; I wanted to believe in the good we could do to each other, not the harm . . . oh, but her bruised eyes, her slack mouth; I wanted to be with her and comfort her, not to be with him and his . . . rag and bone shop. But then, looking at him, I thought he looked pale and down himself, sinking down, almost shrinking down in his chair, and I wondered what had brought him here to drink alone, and how sad it was how pleased he'd been to see me – just an acquaintance, really, but one who would let him be himself, sometimes. Another wounded soldier, with a quiet desperation behind his gallantry . . . and perhaps he was feeling that she'd seen it at a glance, that nasty, sullen Polish girl, and had spurned him with contempt. At least I could try to meet him somewhere near where he wanted to be, just so he wouldn't feel he was the only one who had taken his clothes off at a party, so to speak.

89

'I remember wanting to hurt Laura,' I said. 'Physically, I mean. Thought I never did. Not physically. But I remember wanting to. And my friend Muriel has a pretty firm line on male violence to women. She would say that what that little Charlie Chaplin man goes in for, random mutilation, rape and murder committed on strangers, just because they're women; she'd say that was just male behaviour placed at one end of a continuous spectrum. Like, like batting averages or something. Everyone scores, but a few score exceptionally high. Almost the reverse of your hypothesis about the sex criminal doing the unspeakable thing so that we don't have to. According to Muriel all men are sex criminals, it's just that some go further than others. All men, she would argue, want to hurt women just because they're women, and do; but the majority just hurt the women they know best, in ways that fall short of indictable offences, or at least are not reported to the police as indictable offences. Raping wives and girlfriends, for example . . . Look, I have to go and get some cigarettes.'

'Smoke these,' he said, pushing a packet of Marlboros across. And then, in an odd small voice, 'Have you done any of that yourself, Charlie?'

I said, 'Jesus, Mike,' and stood up, hoping I'd indicated I had reached my limit.

'*Smoke these*,' he said.

'They're too strong for me, they make me cough. And I want a piss. All right?' He didn't answer, and I walked over to the bar and told the man with the moustache I wanted to speak to Viola.

'I'm glad you came, I wanted to talk to you,' she said.

'What's the matter? Look, can we go somewhere?'

'Not now,' she said. 'It's the man you met. He gave me a bad time last night. I told him about you, and some other things. I had to. I don't want to go back there, but nowhere to go.'

'Stay at my place,' I said.

She bit her lip. 'I don't know.'

'What time d'you finish?'

'I don't know . . . maybe half one?'

'I'll come back then and wait for you outside. If you don't want to come with me I won't be angry.'

'Thank you,' she said. 'I think you're a nice man.' But she sounded doubtful about it.

I went and pissed and went back to the table. 'OK, I'll smoke yours,' I said. He seemed to have got the message now, and said nothing more about the nasty things men do to women; nor did he refer to my conversation with Viola at the bar. Instead, he became quite entertaining and informative about an epidemic of herpes at the headquarters of the local building society. And we finished the bottle and fucked off home like a couple of good blokes.

I didn't hear her coming down the stairs and she was in the car before I had realized she was there.

'Yes, please, I would like to stay with you,' she said. 'But just to sleep, I feel so bad. Is this OK for you, can you cope?'

'Yes, of course,' I said. Anything was OK for me. I wanted to take care of her.

She didn't speak at all on the short journey back to the flat, just lay back against the seat with her eyes shut, and I thought she would want to go straight to bed; but when we got inside, she was too nervous to sit still. I made her some coffee and poured myself a Scotch and opened a bottle of wine for her in case she wanted any. She said she didn't want to drink anything, but she drank three glasses very quickly without seeming to notice what she was doing, then went very pale and ran into the bathroom. She was shivering when she came back, and her breath smelt of vomit and my toothpaste; I got the duvet off the bed and put it round her and she leant againt me on the sofa shivering and talking in fragments.

She had been out when he got back, the Man with the Shelves, and when she came into the house he had taken everything out of all the drawers and cupboards, all her private stuff, pouring over it like a mad detective. He started straight in on her and went on until six in the morning. 'Seventeen hours of psycho-terror.' Till, in the last two hours, as the light brightened and people started to come out on to the street and the bangers started wheezing into life, she told him all the things he was desperate to know and desperate not to know. She didn't really need to tell me what it had been like, because I had been there myself; I had been a mad detective in my time. But I was happy that it was me she wanted to tell, and very happy to be there with her on the sofa as she spilled out her fragments, now and then kissing me on the cheek, almost absent-mindedly.

In telling me what he had made her tell him, she was, of course, telling me as well, though this didn't seem to occur to her; or rather, it didn't seem to occur to her that what she told me would be a problem for me. And it wasn't, then. After all, I had conquered sexual jealousy, hadn't I? (They don't do these things to hurt us, they do these things for themselves, because they want to or have to. Hurting is something we do to ourselves. If we don't like it, we can choose not to be hurt. Difficult, especially at first, but possible. The only thing that really counts is that *when they're with us they're with us*. It really works. Have *you* tried it? Try it. Sometimes it works.) And of course, I was hearing these things at the right time, when it was all so fresh and new to me, when she was so fresh and new to me. And she trusted me; whether she had meant to or not, she was letting herself be Wholly Known. She was telling me as if I were one of her sisters, letting me see her all pale and droopy and watery-eyed, with her breath smelling of her vomit and my toothpaste, strung out and exhausted. She was with me, and she was with me.

She had never, since she was fourteen years old, been faithful to anyone, in the narrow sense in which most people use that word. For some years now she had not even tried to be. And this had, of course, always been a problem for other people. For her, as well. She was impulsive and made bad mistakes with men, though not with women. I had, it seems, been right in my intuition that 'now I just use men' was more a hope than a habit. She had always tended towards the men who could do her harm; and she had harmed them too. In the two years she had been with the Man with the Shelves there had been three other men, not counting me, two gone and one on the way out; and five women, three of them brief, happy whirls, the other two close friendships, sometimes sexual and sometimes not, both of them still going on and likely to last.

'My life,' she said. 'The big disaster.'

I could see she was beginning to cheer up.

We went to bed and slept the rest of the night, as intimate and chaste as sisters. Unused to having someone in my bed again, I woke several times, briefly, when I turned over and touched her. Each time, she was sound asleep, lying flat on her face; she had pushed the pillow on to the floor. I felt so happy, you know, just to see her there, touch her. Smell her.

I slept until eight, which is late for me, and when I woke she was smiling at me. Her eyes looked bright and clear. 'I had a brilliant sleep,' she said. 'Thank you.'

'It was a pleasure, believe me,' I said.

'Good,' she said. Then she grinned, slithered down the bed, and took me in her mouth.

93

'Hey,' I said. 'You don't have to do this, you know.'

'Want to. Want to. Like it,' she said indistinctly. She released me for a moment and squinted up at me. 'Kiss of life,' she said. 'Just lie still. Go to sleep if you like. I'm in charge of this.'

So I stroked her black hair and held her soft cheeks and her little ears between my hands and felt her small breasts press against my knees, loving it, and feeling oddly lonely at the same time, thinking how good it was to be taken charge of; then nothing, nothing but floating and flying in her, coming back with my fingers on her throat, feeling her swallow me.

She came up smiling and kissed me, putting her tongue in my mouth so that I could taste myself. 'Good, eh?'

'Well . . . not bad.'

'I tell you something,' she said. 'You have a very good taste and a very good smell for me.'

'Thank you,' I said. 'Look, um . . . what about you?'

She was lying full length on me, her elbows on my chest, smiling. 'No, nothing today, thank you!' she said brightly, as if I were the milkman. Then she frowned. 'I don't know what I'm going to do.'

'About the Man with the Shelves, you mean?'

'I don't want to go back there any more.'

'Stay here with me,' I said. 'Please.'

She frowned again. 'No,' she said. 'Too soon for that. And so many problems.'

'What problems?' I couldn't think of any problems.

'I don't know if you can really cope with me,' she said. 'You seem as if you can, but I don't know. And, um . . . I would want to see other people, you know, and I don't like to do that here. And I don't think you would like that. And I need to think about you some more, and you need to think about me. I don't think I'm a good person for you.'

'Yes, you are,' I said.

'Very bad track record with men. Eighteen months, two years.'

'Just the wrong sort of man,' I said.

'And you're the right sort? I don't know. Listen, Charlie, this is not your problem. I'll be all right. I can stay with Alicia . . . even Marek. Marek would want to fuck me, and I don't like him that way, so he would sulk, but he would put up with it. And Alicia, she's a bit jealous. Really, what I want is place of my own, but no money.'

'Well, look,' I said. 'Let me help you. I've got more money than I know what to do with.'

'No,' she said. 'I don't want to be owing you, or I'll start not to like you. I'll go to Alicia just for now. Get some things from the house and go to Alicia.'

'Would you like me to come with you? When you get your things?'

'No,' she said. 'Better if you're not there. I'll phone you this evening, are you in?'

'Yes,' I said. If she was going to phone, I was going to be in.

'OK.' Her little singsong.

As soon as I got into the office that morning, I phoned a slightly jugular client of mine who had a flat to sell for forty grand, and who was in a savage temper because his purchaser had backed out two days before exchange on some feeble pretext – dogs barking next door or something. I told him I had been approached by a cash purchaser with thirty-five k who would not only exchange but complete in two days flat, no agent's fee to pay, and I would waive my own fee as I owed them both a favour. (Yes, I know *your* solicitor takes six weeks at the least to do a conveyancing, but that's because he finds conveyancing as boring as I do, and you and your purchaser haven't got any money to spend. If you've got some money and you know what you're doing, a two-day completion is a doddle. Also, to be fair, I knew the search and survey was all right on this one.) Anyway, that's what I told the jugular chap.

He thought about it for ten seconds then told me that if this cash purchaser would go up to thirty-seven, with completion in two days an absolute condition, we had a deal. I said that as it happened the purchaser was sitting in my office, and I would put it to him. I put it to him and he turned out to be agreeable. So I told the vendor he could come in the next afternoon with the keys and collect his cheque. And sat back feeling like an impulsive, kind and clever person.

Impulsive, though not recklessly so, not by a long way. The flat was worth forty grand of anyone's money, and with the M40 extension under way, might well be worth seventy in a year's time. Not exactly quixotically kind, either. I wasn't thinking of giving the flat to Viola, just letting her live in it rent free, if that was what she wanted to do. And if that was what she wanted, the main beneficiary of my kindness would be myself. Not all that clever, either, I hear you saying: with that sort of money and those sorts of contacts, we could all be so clever, no sweat. Quite. And looked at with hindsight, perhaps not clever at all.

Still. It's nice to feel nice, now and then. And I did, I really did, want to please her and to see her smile.

It's funny stuff, money. When you haven't got any, nobody will let you have any. When you have more than you need, people keep trying to give you more of it all the time.

Steve Kerridge is a case in point. I had a lunch date with him that day. He'd phoned up the day before to say he'd be in the area, closing down a subsidiary and giving most of its top management the chop. He still liked to do his own sacking, having been sacked a good few times himself. I've known him since we were both first year undergraduates, reading law at King's College, London. God knows why he's the only one I kept in touch with, since we never seem sure why we like each other, or even whether we do like each other. Laura and Vivien kept it going for a long time, of course, but after Vivien left Steve and after Laura, much later, left me, we still found ourselves phoning up now and then and meeting for a few drinks or a meal. Still do. I think he likes to measure his progress by my lack of it; and I always like to hear his stuff and think how very different from me he really is; we'd seemed so similar all those years ago, when I'd sometimes go down and stay with him in the vacations and we'd drive his dad's car down to the seaside and chat up girls, usually without success.

Even then he'd talked about wanting to be a millionaire, but none of us had taken that seriously. I don't think he did, then. But after he got his First he went and qualified as an accountant, which I thought was an incredibly boring thing to do, then got into information systems, which most of us had never heard of, and joined a firm of management consultants till he found a car component manufacturer he fancied turning round himself. Did that, sold out, set up on his own in management consultancy. Around that time he was head-hunted by a huge American outfit, who tested him for two extremely annoying days, he said, and then told him he had an IQ in the hundred and eighties and an aggression quotient that went right off the scale: they were sorry, they said, but the only job he'd be right for was president of the corporation and they already had one of those. Then he did join a multinational, an organization so big that he found himself negotiating with opposition parties and people who destabilized governments, the point of this being that the new lot would put their agrarian reforms into action and their countries into a crippling debt problem by buying total irrigation systems from Steve. But then Third World debt became a bit of a problem area, and it was convenient for the organization to finger Steve as the Man Who Went Too Far, so they gave him the boot. He didn't mind, he said; he was sick of going round everywhere in bullet-proof cars full of garlicky body-guards. He fooled around in the City for six months and made himself a hundred thousand. Then he joined quite a small boiler firm, part of a much bigger consor-tium, turned it into the market leader, and after a year led a successful management buy-out. A few years ago he went public. He seemed almost childishly keen that I should buy a few shares, so I did for old times' sake, and saw them rise in a week to twelve times their face value. So did Steve's of course, which made him worth several millions. I don't really understand money at all.

Steve understands it, and is very good at making it, but I don't really think he cares about it. He was much more interested in winning, in making things work, in making it possible to make things and then sell them. Now he has so much money he can't think of much to do with it, except using it to make more things work for him. He eats a lot and drinks a lot, but there's a limit to what you can spend on that. Vivien got into the hang of spending money: houses, clothes, works of art, all that. Steve let her get on with it, and everything else, until she met a fellow in an art gallery who disturbed her as a person. ('He disturbs me as a person, Laura,' she said, tossing back a monster gin and tonic in our kitchen while Steve was having a slash upstairs. 'I haven't been disturbed as a person since nineteen sixty-three.') And she went off in some style with the fellow, a not tremendously assiduous art historian, to live in Florence.

We were all set to be very sympathetic and supportive, but Steve didn't seem to feel sorry for himself. He got a housekeeper to cook his scrambled eggs and sausages and do whatever else he needed, and otherwise carried on the same as ever. He had always been in the habit of knocking off the odd tottie, as he put it, but I don't think he is interested in women at all really. A bit later on, Laura told me that she felt she had to make a full commitment to her chap: it seemed that she, too, had been more 'disturbed as a person' than I had thought. I sometimes think that it was Vivien who blazed the trail for her, as it were. Anyway, Steve and I had things in common, have things in common, though we felt, feel, differently about them.

We met in Bulganin's, where we often go. They have a lot of good wine there at a very modest mark-up, and they are not too bothered by Steve's rather noisy way of conducting himself, being rather noisy people themselves. Bulganin used to be a wrestler, and photographs of him strangling and jumping on other chaps adorn the walls. He is convinced, or pretends to be convinced, that Steve is another ex-wrestler; and when he has had a few drinks he tends to give Steve rib-cracking bear hugs and challenge him to arm-wrestling bouts. Steve, incidentally, is a big man, run spectacularly to fat. He has to sit so far away from the table that he can hardly reach his plate. Laura and I often used to speculate about Steve's totties: they would have to be extremely fond of a treat to take him on.

When Steve and Bulganin has finished shouting the odds about the wine (it took ages before they settled on a menacing Bulgarian, weighing in at an improbable 14.5 degrees) and ordered some food (ten seconds flat: Transylvanian Mixed Grill for two) I asked him how the sacking had gone.

'Oh, not bad,' he said. 'One cried, one got stroppy, the rest of them took it with glum resignation. Told them it was the best thing that could happen to them, getting the boot from a job that was going nowhere anyway, but they didn't seem convinced.'

'Well, not everyone's like you,' I said.

'No, that's true. I suppose it would be a bloody strange world if they were. But honestly, Charlie. What terrible people. Some of them were too thick to be employable, and the rest were too idle. In point of fact most of them were thick *and* idle. Tried to get that across to them as well, with little success. Very lowering.'

'You're too sensitive, Steve,' I said.

He laughed. 'I am, as you know, about as sensitive as a goddam toilet seat, J. D. Salinger, *Catcher in the Rye*, except when it comes to the embarrassing short-comings of British management. Mind you, the Americans are just as bad, and the French are worse. Germans are not bad but I can't bear bloody Germans, as you know. Some of the Germans I have to deal with have *beards*, Charlie. They smoke bloody *pipes* with *lids* on. They try to talk to me about culture, that's what they *call* it, *culture*. Jesus *Christ!*'

He had worked himself up into one of his instant rages, and Bulganin came and hovered about, grinning, sensing the possibility of a bit of fun. (He had once been able to demonstrate the Heimlich manoeuvre on Steve, propelling a lump of rump steak out of his gullet five or six yards across the room, where it landed in some poor woman's brandy.) Steve saw him out of the corner of his eye, and simmered down a bit. 'I wish you'd come and work for me, Charlie. With me. *With* me. You're clever, well clever enough, and you work fast, and you like a laugh. I'm so tired of talking to thickies.'

'I'm OK where I am, really, Steve,' I said, as I always say when he starts this line. 'I like the law.'

'I hate it,' he said. 'Mind you, English law isn't as

bad as Swedish law. D'you know, I think I hate Swedes more than I hate Germans, now I come to think about it.' And he launched into the story of what he'd been doing last week, which was buying up a Swedish manufacturer of wood-fired stoves, because he wanted to acquire their patents and then close them down and make the stoves better and cheaper in England, as part of what he sees as his one-man campaign to make Britain great again. (He despises the current government; sees them as being as thick as planks and not nearly idle enough.) He also saw it as his duty to bugger the Swedes about a bit in his own modest way – time somebody did; they're smug and dull and self-satisfied and irritating, always spoiling his Continental holidays by being so suave and polite and well-dressed and highly educated and speaking six languages and trying to make him look like a coarse yobo, which he might well be, but it was none of their bloody business if he was and he was perfectly able to make a prat of himself without their assistance, thank you very much indeed.

Well, he'd thought screwing these Swedes would be a doddle and would take about an hour and a half, but then they'd sprung all this Swedish law on him, yards of it, which they confidently hoped would enable them to screw *him*. No way. But instead of it taking him an hour and a half, it had taken him a day and a half; first learning the bloody stuff, then seeing how to use it, then socking it to them.

'They didn't realize I was such a bloody good lawyer, Charlie, that was the beauty of it. But, honestly, a day and a half stuck in a room with a bunch of Max von Sydows and Erland Whatsisnames in grey suits, all talking in that bloody silly accent; what was it it reminded me of? Yes, *nursery* rhymes, as if they were trying to bounce me in their bloody laps . . . ' (I enjoyed visualizing this) '. . . clap *hands*, clap *hands*, for *Daddy* to *come* . . . and not a suspicion of a drink about the

place the whole time . . . well I'm sure you'll understand I was forced to be a bit punitive in the finish.'

I told him about my legless client, a story which he
savoured richly, and he told me several more stories
about life at the sharper end of Britain's business
renaissance. He always does most of the talking. Well,
shouting, really. He was very interesting, and I enjoyed
sitting there, listening to him and looking at him; his
high colour, his bulging eyes, his baroque belly, idly
wondering why he was not yet dead of apoplexy or
massive insult to the liver, with Viola moving quietly
about the shadows at the back of my mind.

When he paused, I asked him something I'd often
meant to ask him. 'Why d'you do it, Steve?'

'What?'

'All of this. I mean, you've got enough money now,
surely. And you don't *really* give a fuck about making
Britain great again, do you?'

'Yes I bloody well do.'

'But only if *you* do it. You're not keen on anyone else
doing it.'

'Ah, yes,' he said. 'See your point. But honestly,
Charlie, what a bloody silly question. I like using my
bloody brains on hard things, and seeing something
come of it. And I think I'm a bit on the competitive
side. You are yourself, or you used to be. Who was it
gave up yoga when he found there was no way to win
at it? Jesus Christ, what do you want me to do? Go
fishing? You've got to have a go, haven't you, or you
might as well be dead. I mean, what else is there?'

'Well,' I said, aware that I was sounding a bit of a
prat, 'falling in love?'

To my surprise, he seemed to take this quite seriously. 'Well, yes,' he said. 'There is that.' He paused,
and chomped down a piece of veal about the size of a
flat-iron. 'Yes, I was in love once,' he said. 'Before I met
you. When I was still in school. Sheila, her name was.

Skinny as a rake. No tits to speak of. Not my type at all. But I was so mad for her I thought I was bloody dying or something. And she knew it. She had me by the balls, Charlie. I was in a no-win situation. I was still in a state when I first came up to King's. When I finally got over her I thought: no one's going to get me like that again.'

'Vivien?' I said.

'Don't make me laugh,' he said. 'And anyway, we are being academic, are we not? I mean, who could love a couple of old bastards like us?'

The next afternoon my client came round with the keys and I gave him the cheque. He looked at the signature but he didn't say anything about it. When he had gone, I told my secretary I was finished for the day. I got in the car and drove down to the university. It's a very undistinguished-looking place, our local university, not unlike the kind of factory Steve enjoys closing down or turning round. A cluster of thirties brick buildings with pitched slate roofs, trying to look like grace and favour, a mess of hurriedly-erected, system-built teaching blocks thrown up in the sixties, and a couple of seriously frightening tower blocks, popular with suicides. I found out where the philosophy faculty was, and ascertained from a motherly, if pruriently curious secretary that Viola Kerenska was, or should be, in a seminar that finished at four o'clock.

I sat in the Jag and watched the entrance, and at five past four there she was, coming out talking animatedly to a short, sandy-haired girl, making her laugh. I got out of the car and walked towards them; she hadn't seen me and I caught a bit of what she was saying.

'Viola, he is going, what can I say, I simply didn't realize, and I want you to know I am really very, very grateful to you for pointing it out. So I tell him, OK, no skin off my nose. And he's going, no, no, no. I do really feel awful about this, is there anything, anything at all I can do? So I give him ten seconds' hardeye and say, yes, Dr Greenfinch. Don't fuck up next time, OK?' Then she saw me. 'Charlie. What are *you* doing here?' She seemed pleased and amused.

'Well,' I said. 'If you've got an hour or so, there's something I'd like to show you.'

'Is this something I've seen before?' she said, grinning.

'No.'

The sandy-haired girl was goggling, but Viola ignored her. 'Well, I have an hour or so, so let's go, OK?' She put her arm through mine, and we walked towards the car. When we'd gone a few steps, she turned back to the sandy-haired girl, who was still staring after us. 'Hey,' she said, 'maybe you better take the number of the car, but tell them I went woluntary.'

When we were in the car I asked her if the sandy-haired girl was Alicia.

'No,' she said, 'that was Sylvie. And the answer is yes, sometimes.'

'I wasn't going to ask,' I said.

'Well, I just thought I'd tell you anyway. Give you little frisson.' She seemed in a very cheerful mood.

I asked her how it had gone, collecting her stuff from the black and white house.

'No problem,' she said. 'He had it all packed up when I got there. He wasn't very nice to me, though. I wanted to be nice, but he wouldn't let me. He said, take your stuff and get out, you bitch, I never want to see you again. After two years together. Not so nice, eh?'

'I suppose he feels very bruised and bitter,' I said, not very brilliantly.

'Ha! *He* feels bruised and bitter!'

'Perhaps he's still in love with you.'

'*Him*? He doesn't know the meaning of the word!'

This struck me as an odd remark from a philosophy

student, a bit primitive and essentialist; but then it was a long while since I'd read any philosophy, and maybe it was different now. And in any case, primitive and essentialist suited me fine; it was, I was beginning to realize, the way I felt about her.

'So where are we going?' she said.

'You'll see when you get there.' And then, thinking that sounded cringingly patronizing, I added, 'No, that's silly, I'll tell you if you like.'

'I don't mind,' she said. 'I like surprises.'

Having bought it sight unseen, I was interested to see it myself. It turned out to be the top floor of a Victorian terrace house, quite a recent conversion. One very large room with sloping ceilings at each end, plus modern kitchen and bathroom. Grey fitted carpets and yellow curtains. The big room faced south west and the late afternoon sun was streaming through the yellow curtains. Down below in the garden two cats were squaring up to each other in the foot-high grass.

'It's very nice,' she said, 'but what is it?'

'It's mine,' I said, 'but I don't need it. You can live in it rent free if you like.'

'And you can come and see me in it?'

'Anyone you like can come and see you in it.'

'But especially you.'

'Yes, I hope so,' I said.

She walked about the floor a bit, frowning and biting her lip. 'This is crazy,' she said. 'How long have you known me?'

'It doesn't matter,' I said. 'I'm crazy about you, that's the thing.'

She sighed. 'Yes, me too. But for how long?'

'It doesn't matter,' I said. 'Would you like to live here?'

'Yes, I would,' she said. 'Thank you, Charlie.'

I explained that she shouldn't feel indebted, that I was doing it for myself, and about property values and sensible investments, and so on, while she looked at me, grinning.

When I stopped she said, 'Would you like a little fuck now?'

'Yes,' I said. 'Very much, if you would.'

Quick as a fish, she stepped out of her pants and lay down on the carpet, smiling at me, her skirt up to her waist. Her black bush startling against her white skin. 'I'm all yours,' she said.

When she came, she cried out, 'I love you, Charlie.' People say all sorts of things when they're coming. But she did get my name right.

A little later, as we were still lying on the carpet in the yellow light, she said something else. 'You know what I am now? I am a rich man's plaything.' She said it like a joke, but I have often thought about it since.

NINE

Muriel thought I should think about it then.

About a week or so after Viola moved into the flat with
the yellow curtains, I had one of our tennis games with
Muriel. She's a good tennis player, Muriel. She used to
be very good indeed; she still hits the ball hard and
goes for her shots, but she can't always make it to the
wide angles and get back for the lobs, and she tends to
tire in the second set. She says she likes playing me
because I never let up on her when I get in front; I
always go in harder on her. It's true. I'd like her to win
more often, but I could no more let her win than fly.
She won't play with most men: she says they let her
win to escape being beaten by her. We have a running
bet: she gets a bottle of Teacher's if she wins, and I get
a bottle of Bell's if I can take her six-love six-love. We
play every week or so throughout the year, and the
bottles change hands maybe once or twice a year.

This one was fairly typical. She got to five-three in the
first set, treating my second serve with contempt,
scoring every time with her high-risk, slashed, cross-
court backhand, while I was mistiming my first serve
and hitting out over the baseline on half my returns.
Then I got my service together and began to recognize
that lovely lazy feeling of power without effort: I don't
know how really good players manage the consistency.

I have to wait for it to come, and as often as not it drifts away again before the end of a match, but it's bliss while it lasts; following it in to take the return on the volley just so, and seeing it skid away into the corners. Seven-five, six-two, with a lot of tired errors from Muriel in the second set; and we'd be in the pub by half past one.

'You are a fucking bastard,' she said amiably enough, as we picked the balls up.

'How's life, then?' I said, when we were sitting in the Morning Squire. This is not its real name; I forget what it's called at the moment, Last Days of the Raj or something; lots of green woodwork and big fans and yards of books and squashy, cane-framed sofas – quite nice, really, apart from the staff and the clientele.

We were drinking lager and smoking mine because Muriel had given up again. 'Fairly shitty, actually,' she said. 'The Screaming Skull has been reappraising women's studies. User-friendly, but elitist and cost-ineffective.'

'*Elitist*?'

'Well, he's right in a sense,' she said. 'Women are an elite group. What he wants from me is a few course proposals. Silly courses for serious money: group dynamics for middle management, that sort of thing.'

'You'd be good at that,' I said. 'Terrorizing a lot of chaps in Austin Reed suits.'

'Boring. Not what I want to do.'

'What do you want to do?'

She didn't answer for a moment. Then she said, 'Guess who came round last night?'

'The Lurch?'

'Right.'

The Lurch is Muriel's ex-husband. Laura thought of that name for him when we were all friends, or friends of a sort. Everything about him is skewed and sudden. His eyes are different sizes and his nose points to the left and his smile is crooked and he carries his head on one side, but people find him very appealing until they get to know him really well. His duplicities and deceptions are curious in that they seem to involve no premeditation. He just lurches into them, glancing at you sideways to see whether you've noticed, and whether you care, and whether he's going to get away with it. He lurched from one job to another, most of them quite good ones, and he lurched in and out of a series of affairs, finally lurching out of the marriage. He's married again now, and owns a small string of free newspapers in Yorkshire, but he still lurches back down again from time to time.

'He didn't even phone. He was just there in the car outside when I got home from work. *I* didn't want to see him. He *knows* that. And then I find myself cancelling what would have been a very jolly evening in the pub with Helen and Ange and some of the students, to sit in this Indian with him, eating curry and listening to him boasting about how good he is at bloody *poker* for God's sake! Told him how very boring he was being, and he lurches straight into a spiel about his relationship with Jan and how *inauthentic* it's become, and if you can believe this, how she doesn't really *understand* him. I told him my sympathies were all with her, and what he really meant was she's sussed him out at last, and he started going on about how much he misses me, and how he yearns for my intelligence and my harsh judgements. So I picked up a plate and smashed it on his head and walked out.'

'Really?'

She sighed noisily. 'No,' she said. 'We went back to my place and had sex.'

'Ah.'

'*And* it still bloody well works,' she said angrily, reaching for another of my cigarettes. 'I have no respect for him, I don't even *like* him any more, and it still

109

works with him and it doesn't bloody well work with anyone else, not properly. What am I going to do, Charlie?'

'I don't know,' I said. 'Keep trying?'

'Yeah, yeah, but it's all so boring and pointless and *time-consuming*.'

'Um . . . have you ever thought about trying women?' I said somewhat diffidently. 'You like them much better than men, after all.'

'Yes, I know, I *know*,' she said irritably. 'But I can't think of anything I want to do with their *bodies*. I went to this women's disco and it was really fun till the end, then I felt like a real wet blanket, you know? D'you think it's something I could work on, or is it just my rotten luck to get off on devious sods like Larry?'

'I don't know,' I said. Then, trying out my new intuition, 'I think maybe we look for the people who can do us harm.'

'How utterly depressing,' she said. 'So how's your love life?'

I told her a little bit about Viola, including the flat and 'rich man's plaything'. Muriel was predictably severe. 'Well, of course, she's right. Poor woman. No sooner does she get away from one bastard then another turns up, puts her in a flat and screws her up and makes her his sex slave.'

'Muriel, I'm not a bastard,' I said, feeling hurt. 'You don't understand. Anyway, you think I'm quite nice.'

'You are quite nice,' she said. 'Nice bastards like you are the worst, you're so hard to get away from. How old is this poor girl, about eighteen? You like them young, don't you?'

'She's twenty-seven, and she's the first woman I've felt anything for for ages,' I said. 'I think she's wonderful.'

'Oh, God,' she said, 'you're in trouble then.'

'I think I am,' I said. 'I sort of hope so.'

'How long are you going to give the poor woman?'

'I don't know. As long as she gives me, the way I feel

110

at the moment. How long d'you think it'll take her to get through me? Three weeks? Three months?'

Yes, there I was, sitting in the Morning Squire with hardly a care in the world, contemplating three weeks to three months of Viola with a mixture of equanimity and bravado.

Three years, as it turned out.

And now I can't. I don't seem to be able to. Grasp it, you see. Deal with it. Get on with anything without. Over and over. From the front, from behind, from the side, from above, from below. Oh, shit. Oh, please. I don't want to be like this. I want to be like the man in the Harry Holland. I want to be the man in the Harry Holland.

I should have realized I was in extreme territory when he . . . no.

Look at all these bloody tapes. That must be progress, surely?

What does it feel like to be Dog Smile?

No. What I am going to do is have one more Scotch, then go to bed. I can do that. It's easy. You can do that, Charlie. I mean, shit. Come on. Are you a man or a duck? You're a *bloke*. You're a *survivor*. You're going to hang in there, because you want to be there at the finish and see how it all comes out. Yes, you do.

Come on then. One more Scotch, then bed.

Easy.

– Charles Edward Cross.
   – I'm a solicitor. A partner in Crutch, Shakespeare and Trump.
   – Yes, I'm the owner of the flat.
   – No, Viola Kerenska lives there.
   – Yes, I believe so, but I understand that after her marriage was dissolved she reverted to her maiden name.
   – Yes, she's my tenant.
   – Yes, she's a friend as well.
   – Is that relevant?
   – Yes.
   – About six weeks.
   – Well, let's see. On Friday December the third I telephoned Ms Kerenska's flat from my office at about half past nine in the morning. There was no reply.
   – No, I knew that she would probably be out. I was in effect phoning to confirm that.
   – I had a present for her, something I wanted to surprise her with. A little Harry Holland print . . . picture. I thought I'd hang it on the wall so that she'd see it when she got home.
   – Yes, I had a key to the flat.
   – Yes, she did know that and, yes, she was quite happy for me to use it, or so she said.
   – I got to the house at about five to ten. The front door was slightly open, which was unusual, but it didn't strike me as suspicious. There are several flats in the house: I suppose I assumed that someone had

popped up to the corner shop or something. But when I reached the top landing I saw that the flat door was ajar and that the lock had been forced. I immediately thought that someone had broken in to the flat, in the furtherance of theft, and it occurred to me that they might be still there.

– Because the front door was still open. The usual form is to leave everything open while they're in there, and to close doors and windows as they leave.

– Well, yes. I thought I might very well be about to come face to face with one of my former clients.

– I called out, 'Is anybody there?' Nobody answered, but I did hear a sound from inside. I had no idea what the sound was. Now I think it was probably metal on wood . . . at the time, it simply confirmed that someone was in there.

– I said something like: 'Take it easy, I'm coming in now, OK? I'm not going to hurt you.'

– Yes, I can see that it might seem strange to you, but as I've said, I do a lot of criminal work, and this struck me as one of those opportunistic, almost casual thefts. Probably a kid, or a couple of kids, who would be much more frightened of me than I would be of them.

– I pushed the door wide open and waited a moment before going in. As soon as I'd done that I could see that the floor of the landing, and the bed-sitting room beyond it, were covered with photographs.

– Yes, I had seen them before. They were photographs of Ms Kerenska.

– No, they belonged to the person who had taken them. Edward Hart. I had seen them before, at his house. That was when I realized that it must be him in the flat.

– I went into the bed-sitting room and stood in the doorway. Edward Hart was sitting on the bed, holding a sawn-off shotgun.

– I knew that because I had seen one before, in a trial.

– No, I didn't recognize the particular gun, I simply recognized it as a sawn-off shotgun.

– No, I had no idea at all where he obtained it. I was extremely surprised. Shocked.

– He was holding it so that it was pointed in my direction, but he wasn't aiming it at me.

– Yes, I said something like 'Let's not be silly.'

– Yes, I remember that very clearly. He said: 'This is nothing to do with you. I was going to do this anyway.'

– He put the barrel in his mouth and pulled the trigger. Then he fell forward on to the floor, face down.

– I went over and looked at him, and saw that he was dead. Then I made a 999 call.

– No, I didn't.

– There seemed to be little point. He was dead. Most of the back of his head was splattered all over the walls.

– On the contrary, I found it very upsetting, and still do. I am trying to be as clear as possible for the purposes of this inquest.

– Thank you.

– Hardly at all. I'd met him once before, at his house.

– I thought we got on quite well.

– No, that's not right. My understanding is that his relationship with Ms Kerenska was effectively ended before either of them met me.

– If you think it's really relevant . . . I feel very sorry for him. He must have been very unhappy.

I felt very odd talking about him as Edward Hart. Viola had always referred to him as 'that man' or 'the Man with the Shelves'. The truth of the court room is a strange sort of truth. But truth of a kind was told at the inquest, by me and by others. Though I was able to guess how he had got hold of the shotgun. His neighbour, my client, had been inconclusively questioned about a break-in at a Redditch gun shop a couple of months before. And his relationship with Ms Kerenska had not ended before I came on the scene, or after, for

114

him at least; though I don't believe I seriously misled the court about that. As to my feelings about him after the event (which were, in any case, none of the coroner's fucking business), I was economical with the truth. I did feel sorry for him. I did think he must have been very unhappy. But I also thought he had intended his death to damage her, to make her feel as bad as he felt, or worse. He wanted to haunt her dreams. And if he hadn't been so obviously, finally, and messily dead, I could cheerfully have beaten the shit out of him.

He had made a will. He had left the house and its contents to Viola, and the residue, an unexpectedly large amount of inherited money, to a sister in Australia. I think he must have hoped that Viola would go back and live in the house and never be free of him. What she did, of course, was to put it up for sale. She didn't, at first, want to have anything to do with the money. I didn't know how to advise her and I didn't want to advise her. If she accepted the legacy and used it to buy a place of her own, she would be independent of me but still dependent on the Man with the Shelves, the dead man. She was very poor, you see. So powerful in some ways, so powerless in others. She wanted to be free, so in the end she took the money and bought a flat of her own, the ground floor of a small Victorian terrace house. There was no question of her going back to the flat with the yellow curtains, the flat he had invaded to leave his blood and brains all over the walls. I left it empty for nine months, then sold it, at a considerable profit, to a couple of gay computer programmers who were new to the area.

Her new place had a small garden, and a green kitchen looking out on to it. The little living room was green too, and the bedroom was red and black and white, rather Japanesey, with rush mats and a futon like a slab of Japanese granite. It was very pretty, and he did haunt her dreams in it. Mine, too. I soon learnt to distinguish, even in my sleep, between the little whimpers and moans of sexual excitement, and the sounds she made when she was dreaming he had come back. Things got better, of course, gradually. But we were never entirely free of the Man with the Shelves.

Waking, hot and soaked with sweat on the Japanese granite, with her hoarse shouts ringing in my ears, soothing and stroking her back to sleep in the flickering candlelight, it never occurred to me to think that she had destroyed him. He had destroyed himself, and he had chosen her as a way in which he could do it; that was what I thought. That was what I told her, too, and I think she believed it. She was all right in the daytime; she was all right as long as she was awake. She was angry with him for what he had done, and this struck me as a good way to deal with it. 'That man. That fucking bastard. He would have nailed me to the floor if he could. He never wanted anything and he didn't want me to have anything. Didn't want to go out, didn't want me to go out. You and your funny cigarette dream . . . *he* was the one who was in love with death. He hated himself and he hated me. Listen, will you stay please? Just for sleeping . . . maybe a little fuck in the morning, eh?' Her crooked grin. 'Maybe medium.'

She needed to be slept with, to feel me heavy and warm beside her, smell my smell. I loved to hold her as she slept, feel the thin, strong length of her snuggled against me. I was careful to hold her very gently, so that she would not dream that she was back in the vice-like grip of the Man with the Shelves. And sometimes it worked. And then in the morning, fucking gently, like slow dancing, sometimes to a record (she had a scratchy old Françoise Hardy LP she was particularly

116

fond of); Viola smiling, covering my face with little kisses, playing with each other and the music till it felt as if we were floating over the Japanese granite: 'Oh, it's so nice, like talking to you, Charlie, maybe singing . . . oh, that's good . . . what I like. You're so gentle, you know, and you really let go . . . you know that man, he was never gentle, and he never let go at all . . . it felt like he was grinding me, you know . . . he reminded me of my father like that . . . yes, more like that please . . .'

'What? Your *father*?'

'Yes, in a strange way. Shall I come down the bed a bit?'

'You mean your *father* fucked you?'

She thought that was very funny. 'Oh, Charlie, your face . . . no, I don't mean that . . . no, he didn't fuck me. Maybe he fucked me up a little, yes? You like that? Cambridge Proficiency, advanced idiomatic English, oh, I'm so brilliant in this language, the bull has horns but the stag has antlers, do you think I am a brilliant person?'

'Yes, I do.'

'Yes, you too. Two brilliant people. OK. Concentrate now. Listen to the music, I want you to come soon. Would you like that?'

'Yes.'

'Brilliant. Have your wicked way. I'm all yours.'

And other times, she would want to be held really tight, pinned to the Japanese granite like a butterfly, grunting and gasping as I smashed into her, no words at all, her face a red blur, until she would jerk her head back and come with an angry cry, glaring into my face like an enemy, and I would wonder sometimes, then, if she was still seeing the Man with the Shelves.

She had had a bad relationship with her father; he had been cold and judgemental, unwilling to give affection or accept it, his approval always conditional upon achievement. She had wanted to love him but he would never let her, grinding coldly away at her; 'Like a Black and Decker with all the accessories, you know?' Until she knew she had to rebel against him, however bad that made her, feeling wrong all the time until she knew that she was right. 'One thing I'm grateful for, with him. He would never let us be lazy, and we had to be so clever and smart; he had no sons, so we had to be his sons. "Daddy, Daddy, I can't do this maths, it's too hard, my brain doesn't work this way . . ." But no sympathy from him, he hated anything like this. "Some things come easy and some things come hard; if you don't do the hard things, you are weak and you are lazy; you can make your brain work any way you like, so go and do this work and let me hear no more of it."'

So she had gone to her room, hating him, and grinding away at the hard things as he ground upon her, coldly mastering them all one by one, then late at night climbing down from the window to steal and smoke dope and fuck in the dirty streets with her delinquent friends.

She hated him for other reasons too. He was a professor of philosophy at the university, and had worked very hard to secure this position: not only teaching, writing and publishing, but also being careful not to follow through certain of his insights, which he kept to himself in a private notebook, for how could they be valid if they were incorrect? Also, in order to become head of his department, he had found it necessary to join the Party, to be seen at all the meetings and heard expressing the correct line. In doing this he had forfeited the respect of some of his colleagues, and that of his wife and his two elder daughters. But the views of these colleagues did not carry much weight. They were not professors, nor ever likely to be. Their foolishness made them vulnerable and marginal and liable to dismissal. Some of them were in fact dismissed, and one was even put in prison. Which demonstrated that they were wrong. His wife was not a professor. His daughters were not professors. He was the professor, and he could grind them all down, no problem.

'So. There you have it, as my idiot tutor is always saying. My father the professor. A fucked-up man. And he fucked us up too, but only a little. Maybe medium; what do you think? You don't have to answer. We were scared of him, but we didn't respect him. And he can't ask for love or take love, so he don't get any love. Such a shitty man, Charlie; you know, he would make us come in to his study one at a time, so we couldn't gang up on him, and go through our crimes and our bad reports. Even my mother! She waited till we were big enough, then she left him. She is happy now, little flat, little job, now she tells funny stories about him to her friends, laughing all the time. Still. One thing, he showed me how to use my brains. I thought, I will show that bastard. So, bad behaviour but brilliant exams. All the languages. I always knew I would leave Poland. I hated that man so much I didn't want to live in the same country even.'

'And now?'

'The same.'

Yes, I thought. Maybe medium. All the men she had been with had been years older than her. The Weak Bastard, the English lecturer who had had her when she was fourteen years old, married her when she was eighteen, and brought her back to England, where he had revealed himself as not sweet and kind, but a psychotic baby, frightened of her brains and her harsh judgements. The Greasy Manipulator with Five Wives and Fourteen Flats, who had run the first translation agency she had worked for in West London and installed her in one of his fourteen flats, and had tried to put her on the game. ('Only occasional, darling, and only millionaires.') She had gone with him because he didn't seem to give a damn about anything, but she had found that he loved two things only: his vicuna overcoat and making people jump. So she took his vicuna overcoat, sold it to a man in a pub for five quid, and disappeared.

Then there had been TVAM, so called because he had a part in a long-running TV series, and could only get a hard-on in the early morning. He had picked her up in the Polish club in Hammersmith and promised to solve all her problems, but had turned out to be vain and stupid and another Weak Bastard, too timid to leave his fat wife and fat children and fat beagle bitch, especially the beagle bitch, who was called Stephanie and could catch Bath Olivers off her snout. (I felt a certain pang of sympathy for TVAM, and wondered why he hadn't tried to set up a ménage à trois. With the beagle, naturally, not the wife.)

After TVAM came the Cold Prick. ('Yes, this is true, the first time I thought, my God, I am fucking here with a *snowman!*') The Cold Prick had turned out to be as vain as TVAM, but not stupid at all, except in his treatment of Viola. He was (still is, I suppose) an academic, specializing in a field new to me, post-modernist accountancy. It was he who had brought her to this shit town in the belly-button of England. Where the Man with the Shelves had come into Guido's one lunch time and won three straight games of chess against her. Bewitched by his long thin fingers and his irresistible cool contempt, she had propositioned him. Her worst mistake of all, so far. But we know all about that.

Then me.

All older men, you see. And when I was not with her, and sometimes when I was with her, I thought I could see a simple pattern. She chose them because they knew how to play, because they hit the ball hard and went for their shots; but they tended to tire in the second set, and she never let up when she got in front and they started to limp. No, too simple. Because of the sweet smile, the gentleness, the way she'd run to meet me, laughing, grab me and kiss my face, clumsy in her impatience . . . and then that leisurely tenderness she had, some of those long afternoons . . . where did that come from? She had had it with the Weak Bastard at first, she said: 'He was not much good, you know, not really, but I didn't know then; he could do it so many times, but so quick, like a little mouse, puff puff puff, finish, little rest, then again; his little pink face, even then I thought he was funny but I did love him . . . I never came at all, not for two years, can you believe that, Charlie? Except when I did it myself; but I didn't mind, not really, because he didn't shut his face up and button up his coat and go to the office like the cold bastards, all he really wanted was to lie in bed all day with me and let me play with him . . . he was all right in Poland, though even then I knew he was a baby; he thought he was my big wise teacher, and my secret was he was my little brother . . . then, when we came to England, he wanted me to be his mother and *still* pretend he was the big wise teacher and I was his virgin bride. And still, puff puff puff, finish. But now, temper tantrums; where did you go? Who did you see? I don't like this, I don't like that, I can't stand that girl, do you know they say she's a lesbian? Blimey, I should know, what do you think we've been doing all the afternoon? I don't believe you, it's disgusting, it's unnatural, do you mean you actually *have sex* with other *women*? Listen, I tell him, I was doing things with my girlfriends before I ever met you and all the time I've known you, so no skin off your snout! You never tell me this before, he goes. Well, you never asked me. And on and on. Why do you want to do it? What do you see in it? What do they have that I don't have? I don't want to talk about it. Tell me! Tell me, you bitch! I don't believe you do it anyway, you just made it up to upset me. No I didn't, why would I want to upset you?

Well, tell me then! So now I'm getting angry too, and I tell him, well, for one thing, with them it's not puff puff puff, finish, you know? And we're in the car having this silly conversation, and he starts pulling at his wedding ring, and he can't get it off, and he's going all red in the face, and I start to laugh . . . not nasty . . . he looks so funny, like an angry baby, and I'm hoping he'll start laughing too, but no, tug tug tug and he's got it off his poor sore finger and he throws it in the long grass . . . Epping Forest, always we were having to go there, I am a country boy at heart, he was always saying, my husband . . . anyway, he's crying now, tell me it isn't true, tell me it isn't true, and by now I'm thinking fuck this for a game of soldiers, so I say, it isn't true, I'm sorry, made it all up for a joke; and he stops crying and he gets out of the car and starts looking for his ring, come and help me find it, so we're crawling round in the grass and dog turds looking for his ring and he *finds* it! And it's like magic for him, he's so happy, but I'm thinking, this is sad for me and sad for him, we won't be together long, I don't want to be married to this psychotic baby . . . you think I'm a nastygirl?'

'No,' I said. 'I think you're nice. You're nice to me.'

'Well, easy with you. Because you're not jealous like my husband was. And not judgemental. Bit of a phallocrat, I think, but nice with it: maybe Social Liberal Phallocrat? And with you it's not puff puff, finish. And such a good smell. You want a big compliment? With you, it's nearly as nice as being with a woman!'

'Thank you very much, Viola.'

'Ha! See your face! Would you like to interfere with my person now, I hope?'

Like Muriel, she thought that women were much nicer than men; unlike Muriel, she had no difficulty in thinking of things she liked to do with their bodies. Her relationships with women were quite different from her relationships with men. Tenderly erotic extensions of friendship, mostly, and a source of uncomplicated pleasure for her. But though they were never a problem for her (or for me . . . why should they be? When she was with me she was with me), they were often problematic for the women she chose, or who chose her. She had changed the course of quite a few young women's lives by following through a momentary impulse, and the trouble was that sometimes the sudden illumination they received was not a realization that what they really wanted was other women, but that what they really wanted was Viola. And there were problems in her longer-term relationships too: Alicia, for example, who was possessive and suffered agonies of jealousy. (Though why should she have? When Viola was with Alicia she was with her, too.) Or Martha, who was political and separatist, and saw Viola's bisexuality not as a gift or a talent, but a betrayal, a kind of bad faith. Martha, who was herself promiscuous on principle, believing that to discriminate between one woman and another in terms of sex appeal was to behave like a man, was enthusiastic (or so she said) about the idea of Viola sleeping with a lot of women, but extremely grumpy about the notion that she should find any man appealing in that way at all.

'People, problems. Shitty world, eh?'

As for me, I was never bothered by that side of Viola's life. Somehow she made it very clear that what she had with other women was a different world, more delicate and tender but less intense than what she had with me. 'Just such a nice thing, Charlie, like sisters. Well, like two of *my* sisters, matter of fact . . . oh, your face! Well, of *course*. What did you *think*? Doesn't *everybody*?'

And, in a perhaps rather blokeish way, I was extremely appreciative of the rich and subtle erotic vocabulary she had acquired in this way, which became part of our erotic discourse too, and hence, I suppose, of mine. Also, even more blokeishly, having met a few of her women friends (she only introduced me to the ones who liked men as well) and eventually her sisters too, I liked the feeling of their phantom presences in bed with us sometimes. Well, bloody hell, why not? What do we bring to each other if not the sum of all our experiences? It's not as if I wanted them actually there in person. I wasn't *that* silly. In any case, when she was with me, I wanted her to be with me.

And she was. I really do believe that. She was.

Then.

I am actually doing rather well tonight. I feel as if I might be getting a bit of a grip on things. Denial, despair, anger, bargaining . . . acceptance. Why not? It was something I had, something I really had, and if I really had it, I still have it. I mean, if I could somehow just sort of list it all, all the places, all the meals, all the fucks, all the laughs, all the smells, all the pukes, all the tears, all the . . . haircuts, all the hangovers, all the massages, all the views out of all the windows . . . well there it would be, wouldn't it? I could, you know . . . have a look at it. Walk round it. Pick it up and chuck it out of the window, if I felt like it. Or keep it. If I felt like that.

Worth a try?

TEN

Some Places

1. My place.

A machine for partly living in. My chair. My clapped-out sofa. My table. My radio. My hi-fi. My Kashmir carpet. My bed. My Harry Holland. His view: the hazy Italian plain, the factory chimneys in the middle distance. My view: the dark side street, my car crouching under the street lamp.

She was always restless in my place, always moving; taking a book from the shelf, opening it, reading a sentence out loud, laughing, putting the book back, walking to the window, pressing her face against it, leaving an imprint of her mouth and her squashed blob of a nose, moving past the back of my chair, letting her hand brush against the nape of my neck, pausing in the bedroom doorway, grinning: 'Went into Next this morning; what a dump, full of rubbish, Charlie, nothing worth stealing even except these knickers – look!'

She was always restless in my place and she was never able to explain why.

2. Her place.

Green, green, red, black and white. She would come running to the door, still damp from her bath, her face a blur, her arms round my neck, her tongue in my mouth, drag me by the hand into the green kitchen, pour my Scotch and her wine, then talk, sometimes for an hour or two without pausing, even if I had seen her the day before. About Poland. Her sisters. Her girl-friends. The crap philosophy tutors at the university. (They didn't, it seemed, reciprocate her disparaging views; ever since her first term, when her eccentric English had confused them, they had been giving her straight As for the fiercely argued essays she pounded out between the small hours and dawn, sometimes while I was snoring and snuffling on the Japanese granite next door.) The squabbles at Guido's, where she continued to work two nights a week, moving quietly about behind the bar, soothing the Sikh hit men and fending off the phallocrat plain-clothes policemen.

I didn't mind her doing all the talking. I liked it, sitting there on a hard kitchen chair, holding her hand or stroking the fine black hairs on her forearm, or cupping her little head, listening to all her stuff. I can see her now, her pale face and bright eyes, and behind her head the glossy dark green of the plant that grew too fast and the plant that didn't grow fast enough.

She would make coffee, but she wouldn't cook. We would go out to eat in one of the places nearby: the Nasty Ladies, the Indian Italian, the Ancienne Cuisine Gourmande, the Social Worker, or Channel Four. Or get takeaway from the Frisbee Margherita, the Video Box, or the Famagusta Duck. Then back to the red, black and white bedroom; candles and Japanese gran-ite. We tried the other green room once or twice, but it didn't feel right.

For the bathroom, see Bathrooms.

3. Belfast.

I have to go there to visit a decamped client who is being set up on a conspiracy charge. Belfast is the safest

126

place he knows. Viola likes the sound of it, and him, and we make it a confused weekend, all sudden trips and darkness and plunging into roaring bars; the Saturday morning he wants to take us to a special bar he likes, but there is a bomb alert and the city centre is full of white tapes blowing in the wind and Saracens roaring about. Paul, my client, is comically irritated at these obstructions to his social life, and leads us down one back double after another, and we always seem to finish up face to face with the same policemen. I am scared shitless but Viola seems to love it all.

Up the Falls Road in Paul's decrepit Skoda, convoys of black taxis going one way, armoured cars the other, every gable end a gaudy landscape full of flags and guns and soldiers and brave boys and red and green and weeping women and blood and words, words, words. A white-faced soldier catches my eye and points his gun directly at my face, his mouth moving but whatever he is shouting drowned by the noise of the engine. Paul pretends to be contrite but is obviously delighted at my terror; as a concession he takes us to a private view in the afternoon, delicate watercolours and white wine, and Paul gets into a fist fight with one of the province's more interesting younger poets.

A lot of booze and dope on the Saturday night in someone's house; people keep getting up and going out on mysterious errands, which Viola says is just like Poland. She is going down extremely well with these desperate people. Sunday morning, out again in the mild, warm drizzle to the seaside, a faded, pinkish little fishing port whose name I forget, the pub full of gently steaming people, the roar of conversation softer than the sawmill sound of the central Belfast bars. We are drinking whiskey and hot water, with the lemon slice and cloves. 'Desperate people? We're *all* desperate people. What'll you take, now, Charlie?'

'I'll have another hot Bush.'

Viola's face, flushed and glowing in the firelight. And

somehow I found time to cobble together some sort of proof of evidence for my client.

4. The University of Birmingham.

A brutal fortress overlooking a nice lake with ducks and dogs. September. A conference on aesthetics at which Viola has been invited to deliver a student paper. Big compliment, apparently, and I am very proud of her. She is determined not to be impressed by the occasion but is of course scared shitless, and sends for me to hold her hand and other parts of her. Pets Allowed in Bedrooms Only. I spend the two days before her paper walking round the lake and drinking in the bar while she attends the sessions. During the night before her paper, she vomits seven times. Seven. A record. Who would have thought she had it in her? My sweet, sour-breathed, frail fluttering . . . stop that. She practically needs carrying to the lecture theatre. I sneak in at the back, fearing that I will be denounced as an interloper and imposter. I am not. Most of the aestheticians look rather like solicitors of the dingier type, and some of them glance at me anxiously as though afraid that I will expose them. Perhaps we are all interlopers.

Viola seems to have recovered completely. She strides bouncily to the lectern. I realize I've never seen her from so far away before. She delivers her paper in loud, ringing tones. It is almost totally incomprehensible to me, but it is clearly all right. It even has jokes in it, at which sections of the audience laugh in a loud, combative way, looking at other sections, who press their lips together tightly. Then she stops, and it is question time. A big fat man with a beard rises ponderously and asks a question so convoluted that he is hard put to it to find his way to the question mark at the end. I cannot understand a word he is saying, but his melody is unmistakeably patronizing and derogatory. I feel a strong urge to walk over to this bloke, take him by the bushy beard and bang his head against the wall for a short while. But then I look at Viola and see that she has started to grin as she waits for him to finish. She isn't going to need any protection.

'Let us try to unpack this question,' she says. 'Here we have a big man with a big beard in a big suit. He has read many books and eaten many meals. Just now he is feeling so anxious, so threatened, that he brings his whole library to the lecture theatre to save himself from the nasty fierce student. My answer to the question you are asking: yes, it's all right to be you. You have my permission. Next question, please.'

There are no more questions.

After her triumph she takes the afternoon off. She is lying warm and naked on the hard, narrow bed in the cell-like room, and I am massaging her back, feeling drowsy and contented. Through the window, a hundred yards away, I can see rabbits playing in the sunshine.

6. Ravenna.

This, as it turned out, was where she disappeared to for a week, with, as it turned out, the Reader in Aesthetics. (See Other Blokes.)

7. Katowice.

I wanted to go with her, to see the dirtiest town in Europe where she was born and brought up; and I was, I confess, extremely curious to see her sisters: 'But yes, of course, they are all just like me!' However, she wanted to spend four weeks there, which would not have gone down well with my partners. 'And four weeks simultaneous translation; I will be hating you at the end of it, Charlie.' In fact, or also, she was going there for a prolonged reunion with a Lebanese entrepreneur who was helping to forge the new Poland. I imagine that when she was with him she was with him.

8. Blackpool.

October. Labour Party Conference. I have to belt up there in the Jag to see a client of mine, a trade union delegate who has been in a fight in a pub lavatory. What is serious about this is that when the police arrived, my client's assailant claimed that my client had attempted an act of gross indecency, and that he was merely defending his virtue. I have always had a hankering to see the Illuminations, and Viola comes along for the ride.

There is not a double room to be had for love nor money in Blackpool, but the twenty-seventh phone call produces a suite in the Gustave at St Anne's; which will doubtless be paid for by my client's loyal members. I leave Viola submerged in foam in one of the bathrooms, and flog the Jag through heavy rain along to the nick, where all the policemen are looking very pleased with themselves. My client is in truculent mood, and seems mainly concerned that the record should show he gave as good as he got. It takes over an hour to persuade him that his best course would be to offer no evidence, assuming that his sparring partner agrees to do the same. The police are being very decent about it so far. The other solicitor is a seedy little ambulance chaser who sees this case as a godsend, and more free publicity than he's ever had in his life. It takes two hours to persuade him that he has nothing to go in to bat with, and that if he does go into court he will be made to look incompetent, and his client, who turns out to have an appalling record of violence, will cop it for two years, as he already has a suspended sentence lurking in the background. The police, too, are reluctant to tip up their prisoners, but as there are no independent witnesses there isn't much else they can do. So off to his fringe meeting goes my grateful client, a sadder and wiser man. After all, he can find rough enough trade amongst his fellow delegates without having to risk life, limb and liberty.

I am by now desperate to get back to Viola, but get caught up in the Illuminations' traffic, crawling along the Promenade at walking pace while giant electric babies flash their neon dummies at me, and pink and green lions and tigers jump jerkily through their glittering fiery hoops. The hotel car park is full when I finally get back to the Gustave; feeling savage, I leave the car on a double yellow line and stumble through the revolving doors, down corridor after corridor . . .

The layout of the place seems to have subtly altered and it seems to take hours to find my suite. When I finally locate it, it seems to be full of other people: a group of thickset chaps in grey suits in the first room having what seems to be a serious policy meeting, a family with a baby in the second room. No sign of Viola anywhere. I find a phone and get reception, who tell me that, due to a sudden influx of visitors, they have let part of my suite and will adjust the charges accordingly: it is a large suite and they are sure that my friend and I will be quite comfortable and not suffer any inconvenience. The suite does seem larger than before, bedrooms and bathrooms and sitting rooms opening off each other, each of them occupied by people who seem quite at home and not at all disturbed by my presence. I ask a middle-aged couple who are negotiating their divorce settlement if they have seen a tall, dark, young woman in a black dress. The man frowns and the woman shrugs and points to a door I haven't noticed before. I go through the door into a room with a bed, a sofa and a giant cot in it. An old man I do not recognize appears to be dying in the bed. In the middle of the red velvet sofa sits an enormous Mickey Mouse. Not someone dressed up in a Mickey Mouse suit. The real thing. He sits very still and deliberately avoids my eye. That is how it seems to me. I feel that he is a very sinister and dangerous presence. I cannot see Viola anywhere and I feel that Mickey Mouse has done something terrible to her. There is something moving very slowly and feebly in the cot. I cannot see what it is in the cot, and I cannot make myself walk over and peer over the side. I cannot move at all. I have to stand very still. It goes on for a very long time.

9. Kusadasi.

No. Not now. Not after Blackpool. Let's think about something nice.

Some Haircuts

1. Shoulder length. Shiny black. Seventeen white hairs. The fringe irregular, choppy, self-inflicted.

2. In an old photograph. Waist length, but still full and springy. She looks as if she is stuck in a hedge. About sixteen, pale and thin, in a skimpy T-shirt and a very large pair of men's Levi's. She had to go all the way to the border for the jeans. It was worth it. She looks half Appalachain waif, half apprentice witch.

4. The Number Two. So called because of the grade of clippers used. Number One is the shortest, just a faint stubble, but Number Two is pretty startling. You can get one from any barber who caters for skins. Viola told me, not then but later, that she had got her Number Two partly because she fancied it, but mainly to annoy the Reader in Aesthetics, who favoured the Pre-Raphaelite type, preferably horizontal, as in Millais' 'Ophelia', or more or less upright but still half-submerged in water and extremely docile, as in Waterhouse's 'Hylas and the Nymphs'. Casting himself as Hylas, no doubt. The day after she had it done, he passed her in the corridor without any sign of recognition, and was extremely upset when she spoke to him and he realized who it was. Good. I liked it. I liked to hold her little round head and spread my hand, stroking against the grain, letting my fingers understand the shape of her skull. She looked entirely herself in her Number Two, but an alternative self, with some not unpleasing associations. Jean-Pierre Leaud in the final frames of *Les Quatre Cents Coups*, for one. And . . . yes, we are trying to be totally honest, aren't we . . . there was a touch of Dachau too.

5. The dark, soft, downy shadow on her forearms.

6. Her faint, soft, dark moustache, which never suggested bloke to me, but animal.

7. The thick, black, curly tendrils in her armpits. Sharp and pungent. Best enjoyed in the early morning.

8. Her pubic bush. Thick, tangled, black, luxuriant. Seven white hairs. Seen from across the room, an heraldic shield, or the simplest and most helpful kind of signpost. In close-up, a friendly jungle. The forest's ferny floor. A cosy nose-muff.

9. Except for the occasions when she went to see Fiona. The ritual preparation for the sun. I imagine Fiona; her short, white, nylon smock, her ginger hair, her sly grin. Waiting for the wax to harden. Only being cruel to be kind. Result: a neat, tailored triangle with rounded corners, like a little crouching vole.

Some Opinions.

1. All fair-haired men are cold and boring.

2. Charlie Cross is neither cold nor boring. It follows that he is not fair-haired, though ignorant people assert that he is.

3. All men who like opera are fascists, and are not to be trusted.

4. A woman who owns an iron is a fool and a victim. Nothing is worth ironing.

5. Most men are fucked up, whether they know it or not. And their aim in life is to try to fuck women up, whether they know it or not.

6. England is in quite as desperate a state as Poland: it just has more restaurants.

7. It is nice to have a friend with you when you are having a piss. Defecation, like literary composition, demands solitude. Masturbation can be just as enjoyable in solitude or in company; the telephone provides interesting opportunities.

Three Bathrooms.

1. Crete

Tiny, cramped, spotless. A dwarf's galley. When you sit on the loo your knees are jammed against the wall. When I shave, my nose is almost touching the mirror. The towels are tiny white squares and soon reduce to limp rags. It is impossible for two people to occupy it simultaneously without frotteurism occurring on a grand scale. Consequently we spend a great deal of time in it.

2. Her Place.

When you turn the light on the bathroom hums like a Boeing. Viola perched on the bog seat in her hat and coat, like a bird about to take off, laughing. One hand holding her skirt up, the other holding mine as I sit on the edge of the bath. She says, this is hopeless, we will be here all night. I whisper some things to her and she relaxes. As her urine starts to flow she reaches up to kiss me. The kiss goes on for a long time. We decide not to go out after all.

3. Kusadasi.

I am lying in the bath and I cannot stop crying. She stands naked at the washbasin brushing her teeth. So matter-of-fact with herself. Just for a moment, I see her body as just another body, and find myself laughing. She turns to face me, her eyes dark and puffy. It is half past eight in the morning and I have been drinking raki on the balcony since I woke up at three. 'Charlie,' she says, 'I'm going out for a little walk; you don't mind?'

What does she see? A huge, fucked-up lump of irrelevant suffering? Suddenly it all seems so simple. Banal, really. After all the long, careful conversations about identifications and hegemony and projection and modelling and the politics of perception, rich man's plaything, zombie fucks cripple, Plato and Frankenstein meet Julia Kristeva and Andrea Dworkin, the truth is that she doesn't get off on my smell any more and I am still hooked on hers. This makes me smile, and she smiles back at me. It's not her fucking fault, is it? 'Listen,' she says, 'It isn't going to feel like this for ever, I think.'

We still have two more days to get through.

Four positions on the seesaw.

1. Early days.

I want to be with her as much as she can stand it. She is determined not to be a dog in love, wants her own place, her own space, her own undeclared hours. I am quite happy with this. So very much better than nothing. When she is with me she is with me. When I go away I carry her with me in my mind. I want more but I love what I have. It's early days yet, she keeps saying.

2. Six months in.

She becomes very dependent, hates me to go away, resents my work, physically clings to me when it's time for me to go. In bed she loves to lie on top of me, burying her nose in my navel, my upper lip, my throat, smelling my smell. 'Get back into bed. Do not get washed. I am hating it when you put your shirt on.' I think I can actually remember finding this irritating.

'Blokes' love is of blokes' lives a thing apart; girls aren't like that,' as one bloke more or less put it. Ha!

3. A balance.

She is happy to see me and happy to let me go. She has other lovers but she loves me best. I don't want anyone else, and I like her exactly as she is. During this period the Reader in Aesthetics comes and goes. I keep my countenance, I remain self-possessed. I fail to see that, for her, things always have to be changing. The time when I was happiest; the time when I was already starting to lose her.

4. Slipping off the edge.

At first I feel only vaguely uneasy when I'm not with her, as if I'm driving without a safety belt. It gets worse. I start getting the cliff dream and the dog in quicksand dream. Little panic attacks in the office. I take to phoning her at odd times, turning up unannounced. When I'm with her I don't feel safe unless I'm in her, and even then something seems to elude me. I keep buying her things. She is smiling a new smile. I don't like it.

Notes on my namesake.

Charles Spencer Chaplin was born in 1889 in East Lane, Walworth, not far from where I was born. His father was a light comedian and an alcoholic; mine was an ironmonger with a very moderate disposition. His mother was a music-hall singer whose not very promising career was ended by chronic laryngitis; mine was a primary school teacher whose not very promising career was ended by marriage. Charles Chaplin's childhood was spent in desperate poverty and insecurity; he was in and out of the workhouse for years, and ended his formal education, such as it was, at the age of twelve. I was spotted as a bright boy early in my primary school, and won a free scholarship to the direct grant grammar school. When Chaplin was eight years old his mother had her first dramatic episode of insanity, and was admitted to Cane Hill Asylum. My mother was always slightly out of control, always loosely wrapped, as they say; but no one, as far as I know, ever suggested locking her up.

When Chaplin was nineteen and a junior member of the Fred Karno troupe, he met a fifteen-year-old dancer called Hetty Kelly and became infatuated with her. Although he was at the time too boiled and shy and poker-faced to follow through, he remained obsessed with Hetty Kelly, or his idealized image of her, throughout his life. My Hetty Kelly was called Doreen Platt and we were both ten years old when we met. She had the sharpest nose I had ever seen; to me it was a mark of her perfection. We sat together at the back of the class and had a shared pet, a green caterpillar. One Good Friday I went round to her house. We went for a long walk in our wellies. I held her hand on the way back. It was our first and only date. I think I must have felt it was enough. Unlike the Little Fellow, I never sought to reincarnate my first love in another. I don't think any of them were like her, though they all had interesting noses.

The Working-Class Hero was attracted to a succession of teenage girls throughout his life, seduced a number of fifteen and sixteen year olds, and even married three of them. (He screwed a lot of grown-ups as well, of course, but seemed uninterested in or incapable of sustaining a relationship of any length with adult women.) Once he had them hooked he treated them abominably, neglecting them, being unfaithful to them, ridiculing and savaging them for their immaturity and childishness, the qualities that had attracted him in the first place. He was baffled, enraged, betrayed, when they turned against him. The women I loved were all very different from each other, and by and large they treated me and I treated them with tenderness. But we did each other harm just the same.

Charles Spencer Chaplin appears to have been as randy as a stoat, coupling as many as seven times in the course of an evening at intervals of only a few minutes, according to his second wife, Lita Grey Chaplin. And the couplings were stoatish in their brevity; Lita didn't experience orgasm until long after the birth of their first child, when the marriage was already on the rocks. (She was, of course, a virgin when they met.) I am no stoat. In either respect.

He seems to have had an obsessive, driven urge to make other people love him, and an inability to love them back. Not my problem.

I don't think he understood sex at all. Still, neither do I. And I don't think I bloody well want to.

He was the great comic genius of the twentieth century, and he had no sense of humour at all. The films, if you look at them, are all about betrayal, humiliation and revenge.

Condemned to repeat the same mistake again and again, at the age of fifty-three he met Oona O'Neill, who was aged sixteen at the time. And they lived happily ever after.

But look at the smile. He still looks ready to take your hand off. Or hers.

He never stopped wanting to get his own back.

I just want to be free of all this.

I wonder how Dog Smile got to be the way he is.

Times when I was bored with her.

1. In the mornings, sitting at the kitchen table, drinking black coffee that was too hot to drink fast, both of us with one eye on the clock, all kissed out; angry with me for having to go but impatient to be rid of me at the same time, she would punish me by talking at some length about the plant that grew too fast and the plant that did not grow fast enough, until I wanted to stuff the pair of them into the dustbin, and her too, squash the lid down on the lot of them.

'Viola, this is very boring.'

'Yes? So who else am I to talk to about these plants? You don't love me any more or what?'

2. Um . . . no, sorry. That's the lot.

Other Blokes.

1. No, I have had it with these lists. What does it matter? There were other blokes, and they were weak bastards or cold bastards, and they were all fucked up. The cold bastards were attractive because of their coldness and their self-control, but they all fell to bits in the end. Well, she was a bad chooser, she chose the wrong sort of bloke.

I once caught a glimpse of the Reader in Aesthetics. He was about six foot four inches tall and looked as if he weighed about ten stone. He was coming out of her door as I pulled up one evening in the Jag. He peered to right and left with his head cocked back, looking down his pink beaky nose, then skittered away down the street with his coat flapping in the wind, like an. . . . He didn't bother me. I was all right then. I could be quite funny and neat about him if I felt like it, but I don't feel like it any more. He made her cry a bit and then she made him cry a lot. Why does it all have to be like that? Why do we have to do each other harm?

At one time I was somewhat seduced by the thinking of a fat old fart called Fritz Perls, pioneer of Gestalt Therapy. This twinkly old mountebank, or twentieth-century genius, depending on the way you look at him (he is usually photographed in a white kaftan, looking like a monstrous baby with a huge, curly, white false beard, chuckling and twinkling away at the great tragi-comedy we fat old farts call Life), is appealing because he gives his patients back the dignity of choice: 'So your wife's left you and you've lost your job and your children hate you and new people shun you, because you're a manic-depressive alcoholic with a tendency to snarl at people and let them down; so, fine, that's OK with me, that's fine, if that's what you want. Not everyone would like it that way, but you do, so where's your problem?'

'I never said I liked it this way.'

'You choose to be this way, you *must* like it. I can see how it might be fun for you.'

'It is *not* fucking well *fun* for me! I *hate* being this way!'

'So choose to enjoy it. Or choose to be some other way.'

'I *can't.*'

'No.' Little twinkle, waggy finger, little smiles starting to form on the faces of the aficionados. 'Say, I don't *want* to enjoy it, I don't *want* to change, I like it *just the way it is.* Then you start to tell the truth, I think.'

Old Fritz made a very good income like this, taking on gangs of rich neurotics, thirty at a time, at thousands of bucks a throw in the Californian sunshine.

Be interesting to see what he would have made of my legless client. 'So this is the life you have chosen, *ja*? Lying about the flat all day, no job worries, someone has to take you wherever you want to go, *ja*, very nice, with the hi-fi here, the TV there; yeah, I can see how *you're* not here to fulfil anyone else's expectations of you. That's a neat trick you got there; it wouldn't be my bag, but I can see how it might suit some people. What's that? You *don't* like this? So get up and go to work and start earning your living like the rest of us, *dummkopf!*'

Though to be fair to old Fritz (why should I be fair to old Fritz? He never gave a sucker an even break), to be fair to the notion of choice, one might say that my legless client, before his crucial accident, chose a life in which it was extremely likely that one day he would find himself in a car whose brakes and steering were defective, on the wrong side of the road on a blind bend in the rain, driven by an associate whose reckless-ness had been boosted and whose reactions had been diminished by nine and a half pints of lager. He had chosen such a life, or been chosen by it. (Fritz, of course, would have nothing to do with the latter notion.) Though what about the poor sod coming the other way? What choice did *he* have? Over to you, Fritz.

(Viola liked to drive my car sometimes. She drove as if she were playing a piano at a concert, with great panache and pleasure. She had extremely fast reactions, great physical dexterity and almost no anticipation at all. I loved to be driven by her, and was terrified for almost every second.)

Fritz would say that he wasn't particularly interested in choices made in the past, because his other main thing was the Now, and what we do and feel *right now in the present moment*. Stands to reason, right? The past is past, so we can't do anything about it. Looked at rightly, Freud was a wanker, a real dickhead. What's happening *right now*? Make a choice. It's up to you. Are you going to shit or get off the pot? Every moment is the first moment of the rest of your life. Every problem is an opportunity in disguise.

Come to think of it, Fritz Perls is the ideal bloke to have about you if you are thinking of running a really ruthless capitalist system. Here's all these people choosing to be poor and ill and crazy and exploited, right? OK, fine, that's their bag. We're not into that, we choose to be rich greedy bastards instead. That's our bag. So where's the problem? *No* problem. That'll be two thousand dollars. Next patient.

This is all great fun, Charlie, but it sounds like avoidance to me. Wasn't this supposed to be about Other Blokes? Look, we've been *through* that. We could wank about, being very shrewd and funny about this one or that one, but it's not relevant, is it? Because they never really bothered me.

Except the one she's with now. Clive Schwartz. The Cool Mathematician. With his button-down shirts and his flat top and his rinky-dinky little earring. Fancy having to go through life answering to the name of Clive. Or Schwartz. What on earth does he think he's trying to *prove* with his *white socks* and his *tasselled loafers*? Hardly the point, though, that. Is it?

So what is the fucking point?

You *know* what the fucking point is, Charlie. The point is that she is with him and she is not with you any more, and even if she were with you she wouldn't be with you. She loves his smell now, and she's forgotten yours. It doesn't matter what you think of him, it's what she thinks of him that counts. She's running to the door all damp from the bath to throw her arms round his neck, not yours. What does it matter if he doesn't appreciate what he's got? What does it matter if he treats her like shit? She loves him now, and she doesn't love you any more. Don't you *understand* that?

Of course I understand it. I just can't accept it, that's all. Why couldn't the little rat stay home with his videos and his pot noodles and bloody well leave her *alone*?

If it hadn't been him, it would have been someone else. Did you think that something like that could go on for ever, or what?

No. It's just . . . look, I wasn't *ready*.

Would you ever have been?

I don't know.

This hasn't worked, has it? I thought if I could get some of it down, sort of fix it somehow, I could get back from it. Have a proper look at it. Understand it. Accept it. Was that what the Man with the Shelves was trying to do? All those images: from the front, from the back, from the side, from above, from below, still, on the move, in focus, out of focus, smiling, fierce, blank-faced, dressed, half-dressed, naked. Over and over again. He, too, must have thought it was worth a try. He thought he could understand, accept, and choose what to do about it.

* *. *

It turns out that my legless client exercised some choice as well. The wife's story was not, as I had thought, an entire fabrication. He had suggested to her that it might give them both pleasure if she were to have sex with another woman in his presence. She went along with the idea with some misgivings and found that she enjoyed the experience very much indeed. Things would have been fine if she had not fallen in love with the other woman.

So perhaps that twinkly old charlatan has a point after all. Perhaps we do choose our lives. Shall we try it out? Just to hear how it sounds?

I can't feel any other way . . . no. I *don't want to feel* any other way than the way I feel. I enjoy hurting like this.

And I want to hurt other people.

Eleven

I'VE JUST BEEN playing back the tapes. All my stuff. So far. I still can't quite see how Charlie Chaplin fits in. Or Dog Smile, come to that. We shall see, perhaps. It occurs to me that if I were a friend of mine, I would advise myself to stop all this now; it isn't doing any good. I should throw away all these tapes, and not only these tapes, but all the others that hit the spot so reliably: the Everlys' last concert, Greatest Hits of Roy Orbison, the Chopin Nocturnes, and Françoise Hardy. And the photographs. Yes, especially them. Over and over, from the front, from the back . . . stop that. Listen to Roy. It's *over*. Play more tennis. You still like tennis. Push yourself a bit, play some of those young blokes, the blokes with the sneers and the big rackets. Get yourself thrashed again by that Australian dentist. Start fooling about with property again, you used to like that, and it keeps your mind occupied. Write a fucking novel. Ha.

Evasion, anyway. I haven't even got to Kusadasi yet.

I seem to have mentioned money quite a bit, off and on. Maybe it's more important than I thought. Most people I know seem to be a bit funny about money. Steve Kerridge, for example. He wants a million, he gets a million, he's still not satisfied. The way I see it: if you have more than you need, it becomes very unimportant. If you have less than you need, it becomes very important indeed. Profound thoughts from a first class legal brain, eh? No, but look. I suppose it gives you a power that you take for granted if you have it, and a powerlessness that makes you very bitter if you haven't. You only have to look at some of my clients. It may be a little difficult to identify with the rapacity of the jugular chaps, but the others, like the client of mine who was apprehended the other night walking down the main street with fifteen lambswool sweaters he'd just liberated from the House of Fraser, you could see *his* point. He wanted to feel the warmth of a bit of money on his back for a change. The poor sod didn't even have a van to take them away in, and he was totally knackered by the time they arrested him. I doubt if I'll be able to do much for him. The local judiciary regard that sort of thing as outrageous and deliberately provocative lawlessness. The sort of challenge to civilized values that must be countered firmly, by which they mean vindictively. Scaring out protected tenants so you can do up a Regency terrace, on the other hand, invokes thoughts about our responsibility towards our architectural heritage. Or to put it more crudely: if you have a great deal of money and you don't give a shit, you can do what you bloody well like these days. Trust me. I see these things at close quarters.

When she decided to take the money the Man with the Shelves had left her, she gave up the translating and cut Guido's down to two sessions a week. In six months she had spent what she had left over from buying the flat and she was a rich man's plaything again. It didn't bother me. Why should it? It didn't seem to bother her. But it must have. That's what I think now. She wouldn't live with me and share my money; she didn't want to be married again, ever. She wanted to be independent, but she couldn't be. It seemed stupid not to use my money to buy meals and go on holidays and buy her things she needed, like the word processor, or wanted, like clothes and scent. Even though I liked her best when she had nothing on and smelt entirely of herself. Or to lend her money; when she wanted to fly to Poland, for example. Lend was the way we put it. She could always pay me back when she was rich, if she wanted to. Or not, if she didn't want to. It didn't bother me.

She bought things for me too, or stole them for me sometimes. And if the things she had bought were expensive she would have to borrow from me quite soon afterwards. That didn't bother me either, but the stealing did. I could never talk her out of that: it was too important to her. It made her feel so good. It wasn't indiscriminate. She had to be in the right mood, angry or disappointed about something. The shop had to be reasonably upmarket; she was too proud to rip off Benetton or Marks and Spencer. The goods had to be, in her opinion, not worth the money asked for them. And once stolen, they were treasured like the spoils of war. She must have been bloody good at it because she was never caught. Probably she did it the way she drove my car – gaily, as if she were playing. I would guess that she was seen doing it more than once but the people who saw her couldn't quite believe their eyes. Style counts for a lot in these matters.

It's not that I was shocked or anything. I was a bit of a robber myself when I was a lad. I could never resist pens; flash, fat fountain pens for preference. 'Still in short trousers, and a phallocrat already, Charlie!' I don't know. I remember the excitement, working my courage up, telling myself, nothing ventured, nothing gained. I thought of it as winning. I was powerless then and winning made me feel powerful. I was caught once or twice, but never prosecuted. These days, I'd probably be thoroughly criminalized by the time I was out of secondary school, like so many of my clients. Later on it was books, the typical target of the male middle-class klepto. I told myself it was because I couldn't afford them; but I always bought the books I really needed. And stole the ones I fancied reading. I can remember the exact moment when I packed it in for good. I was twenty-three years old and contemplating pocketing a *Pelican*. My courage was wavering, and I knew that I had already dithered long enough to arouse suspicion. Then it came to me that I was now a qualified solicitor, and what a jolly little filler my case would make in the *South Wales Echo*: 'Charles Cross, a Cardiff solicitor, was convicted this morning of stealing a paperback book (value 4s 6d) from Lear's Bookshop. Title of the book? *Ethics*.

So I bought it instead. I still have it. Look, there it is on the bookshelf. Next to *Frankenstein. Ethics*, by P. H. Nowell-Smith. Not a bad book. It helped me to clarify my thinking without modifying my conduct in the least. Just what you want from philosophy. What made me modify my conduct could hardly be described as an ethical decision. It was something to do with a failure of courage, and something to do with the realization that I now had much more to lose than I had to gain. I had become one of Them.

Viola never thought of herself as one of Them. I doubt that she ever will. Part of her power over me.

I am never tempted to steal things now. The only crimes that interest me now, emotionally I mean, are crimes of violence. If you want to hurt someone, physically, and you're pretty sure you can get away with it, or don't care whether you get away with it or not, what stops you? P. H. Nowell-Smith offers quite a few tentative answers to this one. None of them rings a bell with me, except the one about being able to imagine the feelings of the potential victim, and identifying with them. That's always carried a lot of weight with me, but thinking about it now, I can't get my head round it. It's a con. Isn't it? We don't really identify with anyone except ourselves. I can imagine myself afterwards thinking, no, that was a terrible mistake, that was not what I meant at all, I can't bear to look at this or think about it, I want to put things back together the way they were. In the cat dream I feel sorry for the cat I have to strangle, but I don't think I identify with it.

'Charlie, you haven't been listening. Of course you identify with the cat, it's part of you; every element of the dream is part of you, it's your dream. You're the cat, you're the claws, you're the floor, the ceiling and the carpet; now, do we shit or get off the pot? Say after me, I am a small, crazy cat and Charlie is trying to strangle me, and if he will let go of my throat for a second I will tell you how I feel about this.'

Oh, fuck, off, Fritz.

Odd thing happened today. George Trump came into my office. George is the senior partner: the firm is called Crutch, Shakespeare and Trump, but there haven't been any Crutches or Shakespeares for years, and George is, rather pleasingly, the last Trump. George doesn't bother me normally. He leaves me alone to get on with the difficult bits and the unpleasant bits, and is very appreciative of my efforts as a rule. About once a year he makes a complete balls-up of something, usually a tricky bit of probate, and he comes to me to sort it out for him. He comes to me because he knows I can do the business and because he trusts me not to gossip to the other partners about what a dickhead he is. For these small favours he slips me a case of port now and then.

Usually he comes straight out with whatever it is,

like the plucky little fellow he is, but today he wandered about the room first in a puzzled sort of way before saying, 'Mind if I sit down for a second, Charles?'

'Not a bit, George.' Funny, I thought. He's always sat down before without asking and I've never minded in the least. Then I saw his problem: there wasn't anywhere to sit. The files were three deep on all the flat surfaces. I let my secretary go last month: had to let her go, really, because she walked out one Friday afternoon after telling me that I was impossible. I said that was a bloody silly thing to say because I was manifestly possible, actual, in fact. I suppose that was a bloody silly thing to say as well, the sort of thing P. H. Nowell-Smith and his pals probably go in for, pretending to be confused by English idioms, ho ho. I haven't got round to replacing her yet. Savouring the peace and quiet. She was a noisy, combative sort of person and I've been thinking that perhaps I get on better on my own. Though I must admit she was bloody good at putting things away.

I shifted the pile of files off the chair on to the floor and George sat down. Then I had to shift some more files off the desk so that I could see my senior partner. He's rather short. In fact, he's probably the smallest solicitor in the Midlands, come to think of it.

'See you've got a lot on your plate, Charles,' he said.

'No, no, not really, not all that much,' I said. 'Don't you worry about that, I can always fit a bit more in.'

He seemed to be eyeing the open bottle of Bell's on the desk and I asked him if he wanted a drink.

'Oh, no, no, no, no, no,' he said, and then, as if I might have missed the import of this, 'No, I don't think so. Bit early in the day for me, Charles.'

As it was half past nine in the morning, I should have thought it was a bit early in the day for anyone; then I recalled that I had in fact had a slight stiffener an hour ago, when I first got in. With a coffee. It's all right, that, you know. French lorry drivers do that.

'But you go ahead, though, if you, er . . .'

Well I would have if I'd wanted to; my bloody office, my bloody Bell's, after all, what was he on about? But as it happened, I didn't, so I didn't. I was beginning to think that this latest cock-up of George's must be a really major one, he was taking so long to get round to it.

'Charles,' he said, 'is everything, you know, all right, sort of thing?'

'Well,' I said. 'Hard to say. I've got a broken heart; I'm consumed with panic, terror, rage and despair, and I think I might be going off my trolley, but apart from that things are pretty normal, I think.'

He laughed a lot at that in an Edward Heath sort of way. 'Oh, that's all right then,' he said, when he'd recovered enough. 'Thought there might have been, you know, well, I've seen some good men burn out from overwork in this job. Came quite close to it myself once. Luckily I recognized the warning signs in time and acted on them.'

Yes, I thought, you acted on them all right; I haven't seen you do more than two hours' work a day in the six years I've been here. Didn't say it, though. He's rather a sweet old bloke, George Trump.

'I'd, ah . . . I'd hate to think that we were overloading you, Charles.'

'Don't worry, George,' I said, in what I hoped was a soothing tone. 'I'd soon start screaming if that happened.' Come on, you silly old fart, I was thinking, tell Charlie what the matter is and we'll sort it in an hour, half an hour; I'm due in court this morning.

'Um . . . Courtney Tench telephoned me yesterday evening, Charles,' he said. 'He telephoned me at my private residence.'

'Good God,' I said. George Trump is the only person I know who refers to his house as his private residence, and his ex-directory private telephone squats mute in his study, waiting for the day when Mrs Trump will make the 999 call for the ambulance to take George away.

'Well, quite. He was very agitated, Charles. Almost abusive.'

Courtney Tench is one of the nastiest of my jugular clients, and I remembered that I was supposed to be processing some bit of Machiavellian chicanery for him involving the formation of a limited company which will then enable him to sell himself things at bargain prices. Not having much enthusiasm for Tench or his chicanery, I'd delayed getting round to it for a day or two. Or perhaps a week or two, come to think of it. And time does tend to be of the essence in matters of this kind. Not like me. Still. Serve the sod right. Ha.

'George, this is dreadful,' I said. 'I hope you sent him away with a flea in his ear. I don't think we need Courtney Tench, do you, really? Shall we tell him to take his business elsewhere?'

George looked shocked. He hates to think of any business at all going elsewhere. 'He's a very good client, Charles.'

I thought of indulging in a bit of P. H. Nowell-Smithery about the special usage of the word 'good' in this context, but decided to let George off it.

'Er . . . I wondered if you'd like me to take it off your hands?'

'God, no. It's all right. I'll phone him this morning.'

'Well, I, er, did actually tell him I'd take it over personally . . . if you're agreeable, that is.'

Christ, I thought. *That's* what he wanted. He's come to do *me* a favour. 'George, I'm touched. Of course I don't mind. If you really feel you could bear it.' Or understand it.

'It would be a pleasure, Charles.' He got up. 'Well, I'll, ah . . .' He stared around him with a sort of puzzled frown on his face, as if he was trying to remember where the door was, or who he was. 'Look, don't feel you have to, ah . . . I mean, if you feel like a holiday or anything . . . Dickson Sands have that very bright young legal executive who I gather is not averse to being poached. Greek, of course, but that sort of thing doesn't matter nowadays. All I mean is, well . . .'

'I don't want a holiday, George,' I said.

'Well, er . . . fine.'

When he'd gone I decided that I would have a drink after all. While I drank it I had a bit of a stare round. The place did look somewhat cluttered. Better get a new secretary after all. Then I noticed that tears were flowing copiously down my cheeks, for no reason that I could think of. That's all right. Women do that all the time. It's supposed to be good for you.

Then I went off to the Crown Court, where we got a very bad result indeed. Solicitors, of course, are not allowed to do the business in the Crown Court, and we had retained Rosie Trimble, who is usually extremely effective. I'd done all the preparatory work. Our client was a poor dab whose whole life had been a succession of bad luck. Heavily into the moneylenders, he had done just two cocaine runs, and been very parsimoniously paid for them. The organizer of the whole operation was sent down for eight last week, and we had reckoned three, or four at the very worst, for our chap. He got seven. For a first offence. The trouble was that we had not succeeded in opening up a clear gap between him and the principal villains in terms of levels of criminality. The judge in fact remarked on this while passing sentence, which might give us grounds for appeal, though I doubt it. It wasn't Rosie's fault. She did the best that could be done with a lot of rather fuzzy-sounding material. The preparatory work had been short on the kind of detail that makes the difference. Rosie didn't say this afterwards and neither did I, but what we both felt was that our client had not been particularly well served by his solicitor. Not a nice feeling.

When I was a kid we used to go for summer holidays to this place called Langland Bay on the Gower Coast in South Wales. It seems odd that we should have gone so far from London, but that was where we went. I think my dad had gone for holidays there when he was a kid or something. He didn't have a proper car then; we would go in the van. Chas. Cross and Sons. Iron-mongers. Go To The Man Who Knows. I would sit in the back, on an old red cushion that smelt of paraffin. The landlady was called Aggie, and she always had a string of little jobs ready for my father to do; locks, resetting the mower blades, that sort of thing. He liked these jobs as much as anything else about the holiday. 'That's me, Charlie, can't bear to be idle.'

My mother was a changed person when we were on holiday, less of a prima donna, more like a kid. She couldn't swim, but she was mad about sea bathing; we'd go in twice every day, even when it was pissing down and we were the only ones on the beach, and she'd be bobbing up and down, up to her armpits. 'Isn't it lovely, Charlie? I'm ecstatic, aren't you?' Ecstatic. I think I was. I loved being in that vast sea when it was raining and the big heavy drops were spattering into the smooth dark sides of the waves, floating on my back with my mouth open to catch the drops and their soft rainy taste. Then turn over and swim far enough out to make my mother anxious, now and then far enough out to make me panic a bit too, feeling the heavy pull of the undertow as I swam back towards her. Changing afterwards was not so good: wet gritty towels, damp clothes. We always went home with streaming colds.

My dad and I would wangle our way into big games of beach cricket with the local kids. He was a popular beach cricketer because he was a natural thumper of the ball, but unselfish with it. He understood the conventions. He'd whack it into the sea or right up on to the rocks a couple of times, to establish his credentials, then he'd start sending up these towering catches: the ball tiny and black against the dirty white sky, then plummetting down while you dithered about underneath it trying to judge its path. The sweet miraculous thunk; looking down at your hands and seeing it still there. 'Next man in!'

The first year we got into these cricket games, I was out first ball one time and I wouldn't give the bat up, and when they made me I started crying and kicked the stumps over. My father went very red in the face and said, 'Always a next time, Charlie; that's not the way,' and I could see that I had embarrassed him. That evening he gave me a serious talk about sportsmanship and being a good loser. He knew all about that. He had been a good loser all his life.

I was very fond of my dad but felt distant from him; he was not like me, he was too good. Worked like a dog all week, spent his weekends and evenings running round after my mother. Never lost his patience, never lost his temper. I knew that I could never be like him, and there was no one I could consult about whether it was all right to be me. There was already so much that I couldn't tell either of them about: my collection of fat, stolen fountain pens; some ideas I had about things I would like to do with girls.

The particular evening I am thinking about, he asked me if I fancied a stroll on the cliffs. I was pleased that he had chosen me instead of my mother, who seemed to be in some sort of mood and was pretending to read a book. There was so much that I didn't understand about their lives.

It was a fine evening for once. The sun had just gone down, but there was still a lot of red cloud about in the sky. We went through a creaky iron gate and up on to the cliff path, white and chalky, with the springy trodden turf on either side of it. Still warm. I was wearing just a T-shirt and my khaki shorts. I liked that T-shirt. It was white with blue stripes. We weren't talking, but I had this feeling that he'd asked me to go for a stroll because there was something he wanted to tell me. But he didn't say anything. He didn't say anything and I didn't say anything. There was just us and the gulls and this extraordinary red sky; and I knew I should be simply enjoying the peacefulness of it, but I was uneasy – uneasy with the pressure of whatever it was that he wasn't saying.

Then he stops walking, and I have to stop too. He turns to face out over the sea, and so do I. We are not quite side by side; he is slightly behind me and he puts his hand on my shoulder. He still doesn't say anything, and suddenly I realize that he is going to push me over the cliff. I try to slip away sideways but his grip tightens on my shoulder and now he grabs my arm with his other hand. I twist round so that I'm facing him, pushing back against him. He is not looking at me, he is staring over my head, his face red. We still don't say anything, as if it's . . . as if it's too *embarrassing* to talk about what we're doing. He is much stronger than me, and he is pushing me backwards, inch by inch, to the edge of the cliff. I look into his face and he still won't meet my eye. Then one of my feet skids over the edge and he pushes hard with both hands and lets go. I twist in the air, feeling the cold rush of wind, unable to breathe, and see the sand and the black rocks coming up towards me in their neat patterns. The rocks look extraordinarily clear and black and bright. It takes a long time to fall and I have plenty of time to wonder where I am going to land, on the sand or on the rocks?

The bad times started one night in the theatre, of all places, in a town about fifteen miles away. I can't imagine what we were doing there that night, because we rarely went out to see things, and I loathe and detest live theatre in particular. Embarrassment and artifice: how can actors and actresses bear to make such prats of themselves, and how dare they impose it all on us and charge us for it? And yet, there we sit, straining desperately to respond to them and make them feel all right, trying to be a good audience. At least when you go to a film you know it's all over, and however dreadful they are on the screen you don't have to cheer them up about it because they're not there any more; they're lolling by the pool, or working on something else, or they've given it up as a bad job, or, best of all, they're dead.

Wait a minute, I've remembered now. This was a show that one of my jugular clients had put some of his ill-gotten gains into, and had even tried to persuade me to chip in on. Without success, of course. As I think I've already said, when I give money to charity I stick to Oxfam and the Dog Rescue place. But I did feel curious enough to go and have a look at this play, which was supposed to be on a pre-West End tour. I was interested to see what the jugulars liked when their fancies turned to art.

I was in a pretty bad mood before she came out with it. I'd booked the seats by credit card, asking for good ones, and the crooks that ran the theatre had charged us a tenner or so each to sit high up in the circle with a steeplejack's view of the stage. I did think that Viola looked a bit tense, but I put that down to vertigo. I tucked her slender hand into my crotch and prepared to sit the play out stoically.

* * *

About a minute before the lights went down, she turned to me and said, 'Listen, Charlie, there's something I think I ought to tell you: I've started seeing someone else.'

'Oh,' I said. 'Well . . .'

I couldn't understand why I felt so sick and breathless, why my chest hurt and something in the back of my head kept saying, shit, this is it, Charlie, it's happened. Because she was always seeing someone else; I had come to learn that virtually anyone she had mentioned as being interesting or nice or intelligent or funny or sweet would eventually turn out to be a lover, or an ex-lover, or a one-off that didn't work but had to be tried. I exaggerate, of course. Slightly. It was always all right, though. When she was with me she was with me, and I knew she loved me. She didn't need to tell me that, and she didn't need to tell me about other people, though she usually did, usually afterwards, and made it sound funny and nice and easy to understand. Of course she was volatile, and of course other people were drawn to her, and of course she was drawn to other people. I couldn't be everything to her and I didn't want to be, and all that stuff didn't affect what she had with me and I had with her. I had gradually come to want no one but her; that was all right too, that didn't bother either of us. We didn't need to say any of that to each other.

'Charlie,' she said. 'Don't look like that. It's all right. I love you, you know that? This is nothing to do with you and me. I've told him all about you and he has to accept that. And now I thought I should tell you about him. Don't look like that, Charlie, this is all right; you mustn't be sad, you're my best person, you know.'

She was kissing me softly on the face as she said all this, and I couldn't understand why I was feeling so bad. Something about the way she was telling me?

Something about the fact that she was telling me, saying things that shouldn't have needed to be said?

The play started. It was bloody dreadful, in a particularly dreadful way: people in suits and dresses incompetently pretending to be other people in suits and dresses, having excruciatingly tedious conversations which were supposed to be witty, poignant and painful, and compounding it all by drinking like fish and smoking like beagles throughout, while we were left stranded, teetering at the top of our cliff, without a smoke or a drink to get us through the next seventy-five minutes.

When the actors and actresses had smoked about a pack of Benson's each, and drunk enough gin to have put them all under the table had it been the real stuff, they decided to take a breather and the lights went up. 'Listen,' I said, 'this is fucking terrible, isn't it? Shall we piss off, do you think?'
'Yes,' she said. 'Brilliant idea.'

We walked to a Chinese and sat down and had that starter I can never remember the name of, the one where you wrap stuff in crisp lettuce leaves. Usually I see something like this off in about three minutes, but that night it seemed to be extraordinarily filling.
'Charlie, are you all right?' she said after a while. I had a think about that. No, I wasn't feeling too wonderful. My head felt wrong and my stomach felt hard and heavy, and I was starting to shiver and sweat a bit. Well, quite a lot actually. Odd. There was an enormous German at the next table smoking one of those absurd pipes with lids on. That must be it, I thought, and I got up and had a few sharp words with him about it, after which he put it out and left it alone. I abandoned the

food, ordered a large Pernod, then another, and in half
an hour I felt well enough to drive back to Viola's.

We went to bed and I started to stroke her arm. She
was smiling at me in that shy sort of way, the way she
had done the first time we ever went to bed together,
and I was stroking her arm, and then I found myself
thinking: *he does that*. I had never thought anything so
specific before about Viola and other blokes, or if I had,
it had never bothered me before. It bothered me now,
and I couldn't understand it and I couldn't deal with it.
I felt cold again, and frightened, and my cock felt soft
and weak as a baby's.

She put her arms round me and whispered to me.
'It's all right, Charlie, you mustn't worry about it, it's
all right,' she kept saying.

After a while I must have gone to sleep, because I
was in the woods again, in the sand, with Anita, trying
to stop her from being sucked down away from me into
the earth.

TWELVE

IT WAS HER idea to go to Kusadasi. I had thought vaguely about Morocco, hiring a car and heading inland, but someone (the cool mathematician?) had told her that Turkey was ace, and she had this urge to see Ephesus, despite having endured dog centuries of terminal boredom and discomfort at Pompeii and Knossos, staring at bits of broken masonry over the shoulders of fat Germans and Americans in the glaring sunshine. I suppose that was one of the things that I loved her for, that she could never learn from her mistakes. But I had a look at some brochures and it came to me that I didn't really want to explore Morocco at all. What I really wanted to do was lie by Viola on a beach all day, see her swimming towards me through clear blue water; tell her my stuff and listen to hers in seafront restaurants while liberally dosing myself with raki and wine; tenderly superintend the tanning of her skin, watching it change day by day, Jesus, she went such a lovely colour . . . and, naturally, lie about in bed with her for hour after hour, gently fucking, maundering on about this and that, her thin arms round my neck playing with my hair, my cock warm and safe inside her. I didn't mind going to see Ephesus if that's what she wanted. I might even buy a rug.

The months leading up to Kusadasi were uneasy. She was often moody and depressed, and explained that by reference to her final philosophy examinations. She had been told she had a chance of a First and this had unsettled her: it had made her realize that she really wanted one, and she didn't think she was going to get one. 'Listen, how are they going to give me a First, I'm not even writing proper English!'

'Your English is brilliant. Idiosyncratic . . .'

'You see? Still talking like a fucking foreigner is what you mean, easy for you to patronize, so maybe you like it; they don't give you First for being cute little foreign chick I think! And anyway they don't like my stuff; they pretend they do, but they are all out to get me in the end. I'm too flash and heavy and continental for them, they're all timid little positivists, all fiddling about with their foreskins, mention even Foucault they are scared shitless; no, what it'll be is, very nice, Ms Kerenska, nice try for a foreigner, here's a nice little second class degree for you!'

'Listen everyone knows it's a fucking toss-up, Viola. Doesn't really mean that much, getting a First or not.'

'So? *You* got one, didn't you?'

'Well, yeah, but that's just what I mean . . .'

'So! Easy for you to say it doesn't mean; you have your little badge that no one can take away from you, and what it says? It says, Charlie Cross, clever-looking bastard! So you can go round being all modest and sweet and all the time you are thinking, see all the stupid sods and I'm the clever-looking bastard; no no no, it doesn't mean much, just that I am official first class brain and the rest of you are a load of shit. You see, that's what you really think but you never say because you are so fucking English; I hate this with you sometimes, you know, that you're so fucking English about things!'

'Well all right then, get a fucking First if that's what you want, I'm not fucking stopping you!'

'Yes you are fucking stopping me too because how am I going to get a fucking First when I am having to do all this *fucking*?'

Then she would stop, and hear herself, and start to laugh.

It wasn't really about Firsts and foreignness, the tension, though that was important to her. The tension was really about the cool mathematician, and we both expended a great deal of emotional energy in not talking about him. The few things she did say about him felt like cold round stones lodged in my belly. 'He's the first really intelligent person I've met in that crap university, Charlie.' I knew that that word, intelligent, which she ascribed very rarely to people, was a special word for her. It didn't mean just clever: it meant someone who bothered her. Someone who could do her harm. 'He's not like you and me, Charlie, he has his life really under control.' I thought, he has *her* under control when he is with her. How could she like that, when she loved to be out of control with me so much? All the laughing, all the crying, all the blurting, all the noisy out-of-control fucking?

And it became apparent that he wanted her under control when he was not with her too. 'He's not happy that I'm going to Turkey with you, Charlie, but I told him that he would have to put up with it, that you have set your heart on it and I am going, whatever he says or does.'

Well, of course I had my heart set on it, but it was her idea, and now she was talking as if she was generously indulging my whim or something. I felt angry and scared, and made some rather harsh observations about the cool mathematician.

She nodded and sighed. 'Yes, I suppose. I think maybe he's not really a very nice person. Arrogant. Intolerant. Not a nice bloke like you, Charlie.'

'Well. Give the bastard up then. I could cope with that.'

'I can't, Charlie.' Her eyes very dark, her mouth slack. Then, kissing my face, 'Listen, don't worry, all this will be all right. Don't take any notice of me, just these fucking exams I think, are you hungry? Where shall we go? Nasty Ladies?'

She stormed through her finals, and she got her First, and she was high as a kite the night before the flight. We went out to a rather flash Italian place full of jugulars sweating it out in their heavy dark suits with their glittering and discontented-looking wives. Viola had come out dressed in a pair of baggy white shorts and a black T-shirt with armholes so wide that they afforded frequent glimpses of her little breasts. She was wearing the feather earrings too. What with all this, she was attracting a great deal of hardeye, especially from the wives. I thought she looked wonderful, I thought she looked like jailbait, and I told her this, which pleased her. I was feeling very tense myself, not because of the jugular hardeye. I didn't know why I was feeling tense. Obvious now, of course. It was with all the effort I was putting into denying what was obvious then; that I was losing her. We sat up at the bar on high stools drinking wine and whisky, very exposed, very much on display. I suppose I must have looked as awkward as I felt, because she said, 'Come here, you, wonderful person,' and gave me a long and passionate kiss. For a moment I was embarrassed as well as moved, and then I started to enjoy myself.

When we finally separated, the elderly barman was regarding us benignly. 'Isn't love wonderful?' he said, without a trace of sarcasm.

'Yeah!' she said, giving him a great big smile.

Later, of course, it occurred to me that she might not have been thinking about me at the time.

* * *

A week or two ago, I was in Winson Green, talking to a client of mine, a Sikh called Dhaliwal, who is in on remand. Dhaliwal is in very big trouble. He is accused of arson and the attempted murder of a distant cousin of his who had eloped with her boyfriend and brought disgrace on herself and her family. Fortunately for the lovers but unfortunately for himself, he cocked things up completely. He made so much noise that he woke his victims before the fire was properly under way, so that they escaped unscathed; he was seen by an independent witness leaving the scene of the crime; his alibi was in a rocky state, to put it mildly, and he panicked under interrogation.

So, serve the bastard right, let him rot in jail? Yes, well . . . but the thing is, he thought that what he was doing was right in absolute moral terms. And he was extremely unlikely to do anything like it again, whether we got him off or not. He was a terrified, incompetent amateur, and he knew it.

He wanted to plead to the arson, and fight on the attempted murder, because when it came to it he knew he wanted them to get out alive. He actually thought that he should be punished for what he had deliberately set out to do. My advice was that he should fight on both, because if he copped for one he would probably cop for both. The identification evidence was weak and there was a fair chance that we could get the confession thrown out.

'I don't know, Mr Cross,' he said. 'I think I deserve everything that happens to me. I am a stupid man; I should have known I would never have the bottle to be a hard man. We should leave all that to Amrik Dhillon.'

'Who's he, then?'

'You know Amrik, Mr Cross.'

'You're joking!'

Amrik Dhillon is a client of mine, but not a criminal client. He is an extremely hard-working builder who has done very well for himself buying and converting Victorian terraces in the less fashionable part of town.

He does good work and no one has ever said a bad word about him in my hearing. I do his leases for him and we get on fine.

'Well, well,' I said. 'I could do with a good hit man myself.'

'Well you won't be asking for me, Mr Cross,' said Dhaliwal.

'No, it doesn't seem to be your métier, does it?' I said. I still couldn't believe he meant it about Dhillon. But why should he have made it up?

Izmir airport is a bit of a shithole, to be frank. It is a military as well as a commercial airport. A few rather shagged-out looking fighters and troop carriers were slumped around the runway in no particular formation, and a lot of blokes with guns were wandering about for no apparent reason. A large number of people were crammed into a wire cage outside the airport building; prisoners waiting to be transported to death camps, Viola said, but of course they were just the people whose holiday had come to an end and were waiting to be crammed into the plane we had just struggled out of. The flight had been delayed for four hours.

It was very hot on the bus. Izmir to Kusadasi takes two hours. We had been up since half past three in the morning. I dozed fitfully and quite pleasantly, my hand between Viola's thighs, while the tour company rep, a rather nice-looking Swedish woman called Kari, droned on comfortably about Izmir and the Turkish economy and what sort of crops grew in the fields. Coming up to a crossroads, with nothing to see in any direction except bare, baked fields, we could see three figures standing in a little group by the side of the road; some trick of perspective making them look unnaturally tall. There was something else that was odd about them too: one of them seemed somehow different from the other two

167

as they wavered towards us in the heat haze. Then, as we passed them, we saw what was different about him: he was a six foot bear on a stout iron chain.

When she had finished her spiel, or wearied of it, Kari came down the bus and sat at the back next to us. She seemed to like the look of us, or perhaps she just liked the look of Viola. 'I don't think these people are too interested in what I'm telling them about Turkey,' she said.

'We are,' I said, not quite truthfully.

'Well, good,' she said. 'When I saw your names on this list I thought, hmm, Cross and Kerenska, sounds a bit more interesting than the usual lot.'

'We are a bit more interesting than the usual lot,' said Viola. She asked Kari if she lived in Turkey and Kari said she did.

'And you like this?'

'Kind of have to,' said Kari. 'I'm married to a Turkish guy. Two little boys.'

'We're not married,' said Viola. 'We're lovers.'

Kari grinned. 'Well this is what I was thinking, you know.'

It was late afternoon as we came into Kusadasi and the narrow streets were crowded. The bus stopped at an intersection to let a small procession go by: three little boys of about seven or eight, riding on donkeys. They were dressed like kings, with crowns and velvet cloaks, embroidered and sequin studded, preceded and sur-rounded by men and older boys who were dancing and shouting and banging drums and tambourines. The little boys had round, brown, smiling faces and looked tremendously pleased with themselves.

'What do you think that is all about?' said Kari.

'Birthdays? Saint's Day? Some sort of religious initia-tion thing?'

'Close,' said Kari. 'Circumcision party. Next year my son will be having this. For two hours before the circumcision they ride all round the town, so that everyone will know about their big day.'

'What about afterwards? Do they ride round again?'

'No. Afterwards they're not feeling so good.'

The hotel was small and quiet and clean. No one else from the bus was staying there. We stood under the shower with our arms round each other and our eyes shut until we had cooled off, then dried each other.

'Little fuck?'

'Maybe medium.'

The window was wide open and we could hear the kids playing in the little park outside, and further off, the yelling and jangling of the circumcision procession. I felt happy and safe.

'She was nice, that woman Kari. I think she liked us a lot, you know?'

'Yes, I thought so too.'

'Did you see, she was looking at your hand on my leg and smiling? You know, I think she would like to watch us fucking, maybe join in?'

'Would she indeed? Well, she can watch if she likes, but she can't join in.'

'Oh, you. Person. So selfish . . . hey! What's going on here?'

'Come on. Concentrate.'

She always liked to fuck as soon as she got into a new place, to orientate herself into it; she needed to come there so that she could feel it was hers and she belonged there. Much more to do with where she was and who she was than who she was with and how she felt about them; if she was alone, she told me, a little wank worked just as well. For me, then, especially then, it wasn't the place, it was the person, her; to feel that I belonged there, in her; I couldn't get too close, I wanted to fill her mouth and her eyes and her ears as well as her cunt, I wanted to melt into her skin; it wasn't so much that I wanted to fuck her so that she would stay fucked, more that I wanted to be there for her all the time, in her, part of her, so that she would carry me round inside her, wherever she went. It's like that, isn't it, when you're losing someone.

We slept, or dozed, for a while, still hearing the shrill cries of the kids in the playground outside, smelling the pines, and charcoal burning, meat and spices grilling. Then we got up and put some clothes on and went out into the warm evening, walking along the promenade; families out for the evening; kids and old men who had brought the bathroom scales out with them to make a few liras by inviting tourists to weigh themselves; and hundreds of Turks with white shirts and big black moustaches, each one of whom seemed consumed with lust for Viola, their hot eyes burning through her white dress, searing her nipples, lasering through her pants to invade her pink vagina. I mentioned this to her, and she laughed. She thought they were just keen to sell us things.

We found a place to eat, a first-floor terrace open to the breeze off the sea, with long trestle tables, noisy and full, and actually rather impressive, with a choice of about thirty starters, and grilled anything to follow. All I wanted was to drink a lot and just sit opposite her and look at her sweet face, but she got us into a conversation with a couple of rather irritating German gays, in which I played very little part. We went back to the hotel and took our clothes off and I wanted to get back inside her but she said she was too tired, she wanted to sleep. But it was I that went to sleep first.

I half woke some time later, and reached for her. She wasn't in the bed. I turned over and saw she was out on the balcony, and I went out there with her. 'What's the matter?' It was cold out there and I could hear the sea.

'Nothing, you go and sleep.'

'It's something. What is it?'

'Oh . . . too much pressure. I'm sorry, Charlie.'

'What pressure?'

'Pressure from you. Pressure from Clive. It's a bit of a problem; didn't think it would be, but it is.'

I hated to hear her say his name. 'He's not here. You're with me.'

She touched my hand. 'I know. It'll be all right. You go back. I'll come in a little while.'

The tiger is in the house and there is only one room that is safe, only one room with a strong enough door, with a thick enough bolt. I can hear it behind me, I can smell its sharp, acrid pong, I can feel the heat of it, and I wrench the door open and get inside and slam it shut, shaking so much that I can hardly operate the heavy iron bolt. But I manage it, and lean trembling and sweating against the door; and then notice for the first time that the room has two doors, not one, and that the other door is wide open, and that there will not be time to get across the room and bolt it before the tiger gets in.

It wasn't any problem finding out where he lived, or getting hold of his telephone number. I didn't want to know very much about him, but I had a half-formed notion that it might be useful to know his routines. He seems to be a remarkably routine-bound man. A nine-to-fiver from Monday to Friday at the university, except for Wednesday afternoons when he goes to visit his other woman. On Mondays and Thursdays he runs the three miles to work and back. He goes for a longer run on Sunday morning as well. He usually sees Viola on Tuesdays and Fridays. A compact little fellow in his

171

mid-thirties. He looks dapper and self-contained. He appears to have few friends. Even when running, he goes round with a slight smile on his face, as well the bastard might. I don't think he has ever seen me.

It occurred to me that I might start going to the gym again and see what it felt like to pump a bit of iron. It felt all right. Despite the way I have desecrated the temple of my body with alcohol and cigarettes, it seems that I am still a fucking strong bloke.

When I think about Ephesus what I see is her, walking ahead of me, white vest and white baggy shorts, black hair shaken loose, long again now, swinging her camera, her long thin arms and legs brown and bright against the chalky dust of the paths and the dazzling white of the endless, pointless, repetitive succession of columns and broken buildings that we have to trudge through in order to have done Ephesus. She made a lot of photographs of Ephesus and I took a lot of photographs of her in Ephesus; from the front, from behind, from above, from below, moving, still, laughing, frowning, blank-faced.

A fat twinkly tour guide who reminded me not a little of Uncle Fritz was very droll about the communal shithouse, and most people laughed indulgently or indeed hysterically; and little subliminal alliances began to form in the tour group: Philistine good-timers, po-faced culture-seekers, brown-nosers, trouble-makers (Viola asked the guide a couple of hard questions and corrected one of his answers) and long-sufferers. This last group was mine, since there didn't seem to be anyone else I could see who was consumed with hopeless and increasingly despairing lust. These minimal bits of chumming-up: a couple of brief exchanges with blokes of about my own age, quite comforting, except that these blokes had wives of about my own age, who tended, though amiably enough, to steer their husbands away from us. Viola and I were, however minimally, a threat to family values.

And then we found our minimal chums, an extra-ordinary-looking couple. The man was black, about seven feet tall, with dazzling white shorts and huge red and white basketball boots. It was impossible to guess at the racial origins of the woman (it turned out that she was half Japanese, half West Indian). She looked like an exotic stick insect in a yellow and purple playsuit and huge sunglasses with yellow frames. We sat together at lunch in the rather barrrack-like restaurant we were taken to. They were very nice. He ran a video production company, she was a dancer and choreographer working out of Los Angeles, and a lively conversation developed about Eastern European theatre in which I took little part. Viola was very animated. Two odd couples. It struck me that Viola was seeking relief from me, and wondered if it was the same for the other two.

Before lunch I had knocked back a fairly formidable raki and what with that and the wine I was feeling very affectionate when we got back into the coach. I slipped my hand into the wide leg of Viola's shorts, to cup the sweet bulge in her pants in my hand, and she told me rather sharply to get out of there, she didn't want me in there, what did I think I was doing with all these people round? It was, in retrospect, a rather crass thing to do. But it never had been before. Ah, shit. Ah, shit shit shit shit shit. Ah, shit, why does it all have to be so fucking sad? Then somehow we were having an acrimonious conversation about the cool mathematician and I was hearing for the first time about how he wanted her to move into his place, or to move into her place himself, and how he was putting a lot of pressure on her and she didn't know what she was going to do about it; and I said that what was clear to me and I was amazed she hadn't sussed, was that she was being conned by some mediocre, wheedling little ratbag, and that a sensible course of action would be if she told him to fuck off for good and leave her alone; and she told me that I was stupid and insensitive and understood nothing, nothing, and she didn't want to talk about it any more, ah *shit*.

And back in the room she looked so pretty sitting on the end of the bed writing postcards, and I took a couple of photographs of her doing that; look, here's the one I like, where she's looking up laughing – so many moments like that when she forgot, and was happy to be with me and loved me. And then it came to me that what I wanted to do right then was take a lot more photographs of her, naked, from the front, from behind, from above, from below . . . did I want to photograph her so that she would stay photographed? I had some vague notion about fragments to shore against my ruins. I put it to her and it upset her.

'No, I don't want this Charlie, it's too heavy for me, you don't think of anything except sex now.'

'It's not sex. It's not *just* sex. I love you.'

She sighed. 'Yes, I do know this.'

'Well let me see you then, let me make pictures of you. It's no skin off your nose and you can see it means a lot to me.'

She started to cry. 'No. I am hating it when you're like this, Charlie, I don't like you like this.'

'Like *what*?'

She looked up at me, her face blurry and tear-stained and bruised-looking. 'You know who you are reminding me of?'

* * *

174

She didn't need to tell me. Ah, *shit*.

I went to Mike Gibson's funeral today. It was all very strange. Not the funeral itself, which was your standard crematorium chapel job. Janet showed up; I hadn't seen her for years. And his kids. Boy of about sixteen, two younger girls. I couldn't remember any of their names. Nice-looking kids, all of them. The boy looked very like Mike. I wonder if Laura and Joe and Sal will come to my funeral. Yes, maybe. If it's not too far to travel. A good few other people there too: Mike Gibson knew a lot of people, though most of them, it turned out, had gradually lost touch with him over the last year or so.

As I had. I remembered the last time I'd seen him, about nine months ago, in Guido's. I'd gone in there to wait for Viola to finish her shift, and he was drinking on his own. Nothing wrong with that, of course. Do a good deal of it myself. People are very silly about that sort of thing. But he wasn't his usual self. Not the self I was used to anyway: expansive, slightly mischievous, a chancer, with those odd little tender impulses. No. He wasn't even blokeish. No champagne. We both drank Scotch, and talked in a desultory way about things that were of no interest to either of us. I remember thinking that he didn't look tremendously well. After about twenty minutes he went off to have a piss and didn't come back. And as it was then the end of Viola's shift, I thought no more about it.

As the priest, who looked like a long-firm fraudsman in a dog collar, finished his unconvincing spiel on the hope and certainty of life beyond the grave, and the coffin with what was left of Mike in it slid into the flames, I found myself thinking about that other night in Guido's, when Mike and I had talked about Dog

175

Smile, and how much of Dog Smile we might or might not carry round with us; not only Mike and I, but all of us blokes. That was the night when I first saw Viola. And now that's over too. Over, but not finished.

There wasn't any formal do after the service. Mike had been living alone for the past year or so, and so there wasn't anybody to organize it. Or at any rate it hadn't occurred to anyone to do so. Quite a few of us drifted over to the Phantom, the big pub over the road from the crematorium. I bought a drink for Edgar, the station sergeant – several of the local coppers had shown up – and Edgar confirmed my impression that Mike had become a bit odd over the last year or so. Less sociable. Much less reliable. Tending to shy away from social contact. He'd been hitting the bottle a bit . . . well, nothing wrong with that, as Edgar and I agreed; we'd both sunk three in half an hour. Then Mike had taken two weeks' holiday and not told anyone where he was going, which nobody thought very much about, and which was why they took so long to find him. Apparently he'd fallen, or thrown himself, down his cellar steps, and smashed his skull. It was hard to say how long he'd lain there before someone thought of looking, Edgar said. At least ten days, anyway. He started to tell me what a complicated job scooping him up had been, but I stopped him before he'd said too much about it. 'Well,' said Edgar. 'There you go, I suppose. He's out of it now.'

A couple of days after Ephesus, we saw the bear again. We were on the beach they called the Ladies' Beach, a long narrow strip of sand backed by ramshackle cafés, the one the locals used. We had been watching this fat, jolly old grandmother, who was on the beach with her whole family. The boys and young men were out in the waves, fooling about with an old tractor tyre, riding it

176

and capsizing each other out of it with many raucous shouts which blended pleasantly enough with the sound of the sea and the dolmasi and scooters puttering along the coast road above us. The old woman was sitting in the shallows with all her clothes on, and every time a wave came in it lifted her gently so that her skirt billowed, and then gently put her down again. After half an hour or so of this, she demanded a go on the tyre. It took three of them to lift her into it, and they towed her ceremonially out on the tyre and then towed her ceremonially back. When they were on their way back, Viola asked the man with the biggest moustache if she might make a photograph of the old woman. He said that she could, and she did. I asked her why she wanted a photograph of the old woman, and she said that when she was an old woman she would like to come back to this beach and have someone tow her out to sea in a tractor tyre.

Then the bear came up the beach. He was with one of the men we had seen him with before, a tall, hook-nosed man who looked more like an Afghan than a Turk. They both appeared tired, and somehow detached from things, and they both walked very slowly, the bear on all fours. We could see them coming from a long way off. Every hundred yards or so the man would stop and ring a little bell, and the bear would rise slowly and carefully on to his hind legs. Then the man would play a tune on a tin whistle while the bear did a couple of slow turns on his hind legs, holding his front paws out in front of him and a little to the side to keep his balance. Then people would give the man money, or not, and they would move on. I was hoping that they would not stop right in front of us, but they did. The man rang his little bell and the bear heaved himself ponderously up, so that he stood a little taller than his master. The man played his whistle and the bear did his dance. It was not much of an act. I noticed how leathery and lined the man's face was. He was ten yards from us and looking towards us, but his eyes seemed focussed on something more distant, as if he were acknowledging our presence but paying no attention to us as people; and I thought that that was what I would do if I were that man. The bear's eyes were not focussed on anything at all, and I wondered if he might be blind. I wondered what it felt like to be that bear, and if the man treated him well or badly. The man had a stick but he didn't hit the bear with it once while I was watching, which was something. They were, of course, utterly dependent on one another, and there was nothing for them to do except what they were doing. I put some money in the man's tin, and they moved slowly on down the beach.

I've been recording most of this stuff in my flat, listening to my records, staring vaguely at the man in the Harry Holland, drinking whisky and smoking cigarettes; and some of it in the office, after hours, sitting behind my big desk or prowling round the room, drinking whisky and smoking cigarettes. But I won't be doing any more of it in the office because I won't be going to the office any more. I won't be working there any more because Crutch, Shakespeare and Trump have let me go. Nice phrase, that, isn't it? You open your cupped hand and let the bird fly free. And I do, in an odd way, feel as if I'm flying free, perning and perning in a widening gyre, high in the cold sky, deaf to the despairing whistles of the Law Society and all it stands for, not a solicitor any more, but just a bloke.

They couldn't sack me, of course, because I wasn't an employee, but a partner. What happened was that George Trump invited me down to his office and told me that he and the other partners had got together and decided to offer to buy me out. The sum that he mentioned surprised me: it was not just fair, it was generous. He is, as I have said before, rather a sweet old fart, George Trump. He seemed dreadfully embarrassed by the whole thing, and terribly grateful for the cheerful manner with which I took it all, once he'd managed to work his way round to it.

'Awfully glad you see it that way, Charles,' he said. 'Because we've felt for quite a while that – and please understand that this doesn't imply the slightest hint of criticism – but you haven't really had your heart in it lately, and that you'd be as glad of a change of scene as . . .' and here his face went all blank and appalled, 'as anything, um . . .'

'Look, George,' I said. 'I'm glad you suggested it. And in any case, knowing that you feel the way you do, I'd hardly want to embarrass you by my continued presence.' I didn't make too brilliant a job of the 'continued presence' bit of this, and remembered that I'd had a stiffener, two stiffeners to be precise, when I'd first got in that morning. Might be an idea to keep a check on that. But then I don't need to now, do I?

'Charles, Charles,' he said. He'd gone red in the face. 'Nothing of that about it at all. In fact, I'd very much appreciate it if you felt able to do the occasional stint for us in one of your special areas, now and then, when you've had time to, er . . . I've always felt, and I mean this as a compliment, and in fact I, er, well, there's a certain almost so to speak envy in this, er . . . that you were one of nature's freelances.'

You can imagine what he's like in court: disaster. He is, on the other hand, always sober.

When I got back to my room I had a look round it, trying to see it with his eyes. Trying to look at it the way I would have looked at it a couple of years ago. A sobering experience. It looked like a room that someone had gone to pieces in. All right. I have been neglecting my work in a somewhat reckless way, particularly the bits of it that bore me, which are, these days, most bits of it. I have not cracked up, though. Oh no. I haven't lost my drive. It's just been . . . channelled in a different direction. Channelled. Another of those tricky words. I do need to watch the stiffeners. There is something that I need to keep my head clear for. At the moment I'm not quite sure what it is. I'm not going to force it. It'll come, in its own good time. Meanwhile, I feel fine. I am bursting with energy. I can hardly contain myself.

How can I be ill when I feel so strong?

I am sure that there is something going on between Kari and Viola. But that is absurd. How can there be? I am with Viola twenty-four hours a day and I was looking forward to that so much and now I have it and it seems to be torture for both of us: me trying to control this urge to dive into her and hide in her, get inside her and stay inside her over and over, her almost unable to breathe for it. It isn't just Kari. Everyone we pass wants to get into her; all these Turks in their white shirts and black moustaches, their black eyes burning through her thin vest, their wet red mouths masticating her.

This morning, when we were waiting for the dolmas to take us back from the Ladies' Beach into the town, we had a drink standing up at one of the little ramshackle bars. The guy that served us was a little ratty-faced type with brilliantined hair and tight cotton trousers so thin that you could see his dick through them. Somehow he sussed out that Viola could speak German and I couldn't, and he started up this animated conversation with her in medium crap German, but still too fast for me to follow, and in which his intentions were obvious; and she laughed several times, and he gave me one or two thoughtful, measuring looks. Afterwards, in the crowded dolmas, I asked her what it had been about.

'Oh, he was trying to pull me, of course. You really want to know what he was saying?'

'Yes.'

'Well, he was saying, is this your father? And I said, no, he's my friend. And then he was saying, but he's an old man, he's much too old for you, someone as beautiful as you needs a passionate young man, why don't you meet me this evening; and I asked him, what would I want with a mouse when I have a man? So. Cheeky little bastard, eh?'

That made me feel good for at least five minutes. Then I thought: their conversation was much longer than that.

Now we're sitting in the cool foyer of the hotel and Kari is telling us how we must visit a Turkish bath. This is not something that she would suggest to all the tourists, but she thinks that we are maybe special people who would appreciate it. (And one of us is more special than the other one, she implies.) There are two Turkish baths in the town. One of them has become rather spoilt by its adaptation to the tourist trade, but the other is much more authentic, and that is the one that she would recommend for us. Women are not usually allowed there at all, but she knows the management and she can arrange for the steam room to be made available for us exclusively for half an hour, so that we'll have privacy. This will cost, of course, but not too much; about the equivalent of four quid each. Viola is dead keen, and Kari is pleased with us. She's interesting, Kari. She's not like an ordinary rep. Not with us. She sprawls. Yawns. Grins. She's tall and bony. Flat chested, some men would say. But no woman is really flat chested. High cheekbones, wide blue eyes behind her glasses. Wide, thin-lipped mouth with a sly grin.

'OK,' she says. 'I'll fix it.'

* * *

181

As we walk down the narrow streets in the early evening, trying to suss out Kari's pencilled map, Viola is beginning to think that maybe it's not such a good idea after all. She holds my hand and we are walking more and more slowly. 'Torture is commonplace in Turkish prisons and police stations,' she says. 'Maybe Turkish baths as well?'

'You're with me,' I tell her. 'I won't let them torture you.'

We take a turn off the street, into a series of narrow, smelly alleys with washing hung across them. All the signs are in squiggly writing now. We think we are hopelessly lost, but then the alley we are walking along opens out into a little square with a mosque on one side of it. There are a lot of men hanging about in the square, and no women at all. Next to the mosque is an open-air urinal, which is being enthusiastically patronized by a number of swarthy blokes taking their dicks out of their baggy trousers in a leisurely manner and pissing their cares away. Viola holds my hand tight. I am beginning to feel a bit odd about this myself by now.

Kari has written the sign we are to look out for on our crumpled bit of paper, and we find the place. The doorway is disconcertingly small and dark, but we have come so far we are not going to chicken out now. It is exactly half past seven, the time that Kari has reserved for us.

As soon as we are inside the entrance hall with its dark wood and mosaic floor, we know that something has gone wrong. Far from having the place to ourselves, we are surrounded by Turks. Fat Turks, thin Turks, short Turks, tall Turks, some with shirts and trousers on, some with little damp towels round their middles, some naked. Some of them have impressive erections. The skinny, anxious-looking man behind the desk speaks no English or German and is clearly deeply dismayed to see us, unlike his clients, who make absolutely no bones at all about how much they enjoy staring at and being stared at by us. Especially the ones with erections.

Then a short fat man with a huge moustache and a proper European suit comes out from a back room and starts to be tremendously reassuring in broken German. We are a little earlier than he expected but everything is under control. The regulars should be finished in five or ten minutes. Perhaps we would like some tea? How very comforting. We sit on a marble bench sipping tea and trying to avoid the one-eyed scrutiny of the Turkish members; and one by one they start to drift away, stretching, yawning and belching. A rather sweet-looking little chap who reminds me of one of our articled clerks comes up to us with a pile of towels and leads us upstairs to the gallery and shows us into a rinky-dinky little cubicle, a bit like a miniature old-fashioned railway carriage, with two little benches and a lot of carved sandalwood. We are to take our clothes off, and Viola is to arrange her towel like *this*, and I am to arrange my towel like *that*. Then we are to come downstairs again. We manage to spend a good long time arranging our towels; but the ways we find to dawdle are not the ways we once would have found. We are so polite and decorous to each other; already we are treating each other like wounded soldiers.

But eventually we tiptoe downstairs, and a thin wiry man opens the big doors and shows us into the Turkish bath proper. It is a large empty room, marble walls and floor, a high ceiling with a large, domed skylight, rows of carved seats round the perimeter and a huge marble slab filling the centre of the room. We might as well not have bothered with arranging our towels so daintily, because the thin wiry man rips them off us without ceremony, spreads them on the marble slab and indicates that we should lie down on them. We do this, and he goes off and leaves us, the big doors crashing behind him. The marble slab is almost unbearably hot, even through the thin towel, which is in any case too small. The backs of my calves and my arms feel as if they are being boiled, and I raise my knees and fold my arms over my chest. I am finding it a little difficult to breathe and my heart is pounding.

'Jesus Christ, I'm not sure I can take this,' I say.

'No, I think it's all right,' she says. 'Breathe slow, relax.' We are both whispering, as if we were in church or a hospital waiting room.

After a few minutes, I realize that she is right. It is hot, but not unbearably so, and it is possible to breathe this thick, soupy air. I am pouring with sweat. Looking up through the skylight I can see the swifts wheeling in the darkening sky. We are lying head to foot and when I try to look at Viola I can't see her face, only the soles of her feet, her legs, her pubic mound with its neat little sculptured black triangle of hair, like a midget toupee.

Then the doors crash open again and two other men walk in. Both of them have little towels round their waists, and both of them walk with a swagger. The one who goes to Viola is tall and lean, with ropy, muscular arms and a hook nose. The one who heads for me is shortish, dark, low-browed, and built like a weightlifter. His broad smile has what seems to me more than a hint of sadistic pleasure about it. He offers me his hand and I take it. His grip is very strong. Then, without warning, he smacks my chest very hard indeed with the open palm of his other hand and says: 'Ha!' The pain is intense, but I am fairly sure that he has not actually broken anything. I try to turn my head so that I can see what is happening to Viola, but he slaps his hand over my face, pulls it round so that I am staring up at the darkening skylight again, then throws a bucket of cold water over me. While I am still gasping and spluttering in the steam, he covers me from head to foot in thick soapy lather and then stands back with his hands on his hips for a moment or two, regarding

184

me thoughtfully, as if he is making up his mind what to do to me next.

Then he smiles, and takes my arms quite gently, and arranges them so that each hand rests on the opposite shoulder and my elbows are pointing upwards, making the apex of a triangle. Holding my elbows firmly together, he presses down, first with one hand, then with both, leaning over me so that he can bear down with his chest and shoulders. The sensation is alarming, but not wholly unpleasant: my arms and shoulders feel stretched to a degree that I would not have thought possible, but clearly is. This guy really knows what he is doing. I nod to him to try to indicate this and establish some sort of rapport. He grins at me and kicks his sandals off, then bears down on my elbows again, slowly lifting himself off the floor so that I am bearing the whole weight of his body. Both my shoulder joints dislocate, and I have just enough time to feel the searing pain, see his broken-toothed grin and hear his 'Ha!' before the skylight goes swimmy and black and I lose consciousness.

I don't know how long I have been unconscious. I still hurt terribly and feel weak and faint, and I can hear gasping and moaning, and I wonder if I am making those sounds. Then I manage to turn my head and I realize that they are not coming from me but from Viola. The tall lean one with the ropy muscular arms is bending over her, and he seems to be trying to thrust his whole hand into her vagina. Then, and somehow I am not altogether surprised, Kari comes into my field of vision. She is still in her blue travel company uni-form, and she is wiping the steam off her spectacles. I watch her slip out of her clothes, quick as a fish, push the tall thin man aside, and bury her face between Viola's legs. My torturer comes round to her head, takes a handful of hair and jerks it back, then tosses his towel on to the floor and thrusts vigorously into her

185

mouth. The thin man comes round behind Kari, raises her hips and spreads her legs, and takes her from behind.

I have to try to help Viola, but I hurt so much and feel so weak. I can't use my arms to push myself up with, but I manage to turn on my side, and I am trying to tell them to stop it, but I can't speak properly. The squat weightlifter must have heard me, though, because he lifts his head and looks over, grinning. He takes his prick out of Viola's mouth and walks round the marble slab, taking his time. I try to jab my heel into his throat but he grabs my ankle and swings me over on to my stomach. He twists my legs over each other, holds them together tightly at the ankles and starts to bend them backwards and upwards towards my head. I try to lock the muscles in my belly and my back and my thighs and push backwards against him, but he is too strong for me, and I know with absolute certainty that he is going to break my back. Then I lose consciousness again.

I've just got back from Guido's and it's three in the morning. I'm not quite sure what made me go there. Viola doesn't work there any more. But it's a place I . . . feel at home in, I suppose. They have a new girl there now. She is pretty and plump and she flirts with the customers and has a nice smile that does nothing at all for me. I sat at a table by the wall and drank whisky and smoked cigarettes. After about half an hour Dhillon came in. He glanced towards me and nodded, bought himself a drink at the bar and brought it over to my table. 'On your own, Mr Cross? You don't mind to have a drink with me?'

'No,' I said. 'It's nice to see you.'

Dhillon is a Sikh but he doesn't go in for the beard and turban. His grey hair is cropped very short, and I have never seen him in anything but his working clothes, which consist of an old, grey, three-piece suit, stiff with stale sweat and brick dust, a collarless shirt, and heavy black boots. Most of the customers in Guido's are dressed quite smartly, and the Pole who owns it tries to cultivate a classy clientele; he would like to cater for sharp and upwardly mobile business couples who would meet their friends over a bottle of flash wine. He refuses to serve anyone with a crocodile over his left tit, for example. Dhillon, despite his shabbiness and his calm demeanour, is somehow not the sort of person to be challenged on matters of dress. He commands a wary respect from everyone. I always thought that this was because he is a solid citizen and employer who gives and expects good value for money. He is certainly a solid citizen. He is built like one of his own brick terraces.

'I'm sorry to hear you're not working with Mr Trump any more,' he said. 'Who am I to trust now when I need a lawyer?'

'It's still a good firm,' I told him. 'Or if you like, I'd be happy to continue to act for you – not as if I've been struck off or anything.'

'That is what I was hoping I would hear. You're a good man, Mr Cross. I have always relied on you.' He leant across the table and lowered his voice. 'And now I hear that you have a problem.'

'Do you? Where did you hear that?'

'Don't worry, Mr Cross, this is all completely confidential.'

'I haven't got a problem, Mr Dhillon,' I said.

'Please trust me, Mr Cross. I have always trusted you completely. Somebody has upset you?'

And I heard myself say yes. And then felt a sudden surge of conviction: yes, it was someone else's turn to suffer.

'May I ask what is the nature of the offence?'

'He stole my woman,' I said. Yes. There it was. I had

never thought that I could utter or think such a sentence. It was absurd, it sounded like something out of a foreign folk tale. But it felt right as well. It felt true.

Dhillon nodded seriously. 'Yes, I understand,' he said. 'Do you want him to be hurt? Or more?'

Christ, I thought, this is real. I swallowed. 'Hurt.'

'Good.' He nodded again. 'I would like to help you in this matter, Mr Cross. Please understand – I expect no payment, nothing in return. You have done me many favours and I want to do something for you.'

'I haven't done you any favours, Mr Dhillon,' I said. 'I've just done what any good lawyer would do for you.'

'It took me a long time to find you,' he said. 'Believe me, there are not many good men, and you are one. Perhaps an Indian discovers this in England more quickly than an Englishman does; what do you think? I like you very much, Mr Cross, I think you are a good bloke.'

I looked up at him. He was smiling at me. And suddenly, ridiculously, I felt tears pricking my eyes. I got up and went to the bar and ordered two large whiskies.

When I got back to the table, he pushed across a crumpled invoice and a stub of pencil. 'Please write down the name and address and telephone number if you remember them.'

I remembered them, and I wrote them down. He picked up the piece of paper and read it carefully. He moved his lips as he read. Then he took my lighter, lit the corner of the scrap of paper and put it in the ashtray and watched it burn. 'Good memory,' he said. 'Like you, Mr Cross.' He looked at his watch and smiled. 'One thirty-five am,' he said. 'Just right.' He stood up.

'Christ, what are you . . .?'

'No, no, Mr Cross. Call of nature simply.'

* * *

He went out to the lavatories and I lit another cigarette and thought about what I had done, what I had set in motion. I had no doubt at all that Dhillon knew what he was about. It's a question of experience and instinct, experience much more than instinct. I have met a great many criminals, and most of them are so obvious, such total hypocrites and losers, and they are drawn into crime because they always get things wrong. Just two or three times in twenty years, I have defended clients of a different sort, and each time I was totally convinced of their innocence, and each time I won, and then found myself wondering later. I had never had the opportunity of defending Dhillon, and nor had anyone else, because Dhillon had never been accused of anything, nor, so far as I knew, suspected of anything.

He came back to the table and sat down. He was smiling again. 'I made a small phone call,' he said.

'Christ,' I said. 'Not to . . .?'

'Yes, to Mr Schwartz. I am afraid I disturbed his sleep.'

Good, I thought. 'What did you say?'

'First I had to make sure I was speaking to the right person. British Telecom is very unreliable, I find.'

He was, I suddenly realized, enjoying himself enormously. 'But you were speaking to the right person?'

'Oh, yes. I told him that many people had been saying for a long while that he was a bad bastard. And now, I tell him, the time has come. We are going to break your legs and then we are going to break your face.'

'Christ,' I said. 'What did he say?'

'He didn't say anything, because I put the phone down. I think, two or three times like this, before we hurt him. It is important, in a thing like this, that he understands he is going to be hurt. Otherwise, like a road accident.'

'Listen,' I said. 'I don't want to go on with this. I'd

189

just like you to forget about it. Will you do that? It's not what I want.'

'Then tell me what you want.'

'I don't know what I want,' I said. 'But not that.'

'I understand,' he said. 'I know what you are think-ing: you don't want anyone else to do this for you, you are a brave man, you want to do this for yourself. That's not wise. First, you will be suspected. But also, this is not something you have done before. Is it?'

'No,' I said.

'It's a very simple thing, but it's not an easy thing. Nobody knows how they will feel until they are doing it. You see how I trust you? But we are trusting each other now. Look at poor Sandeep Dhaliwal: you are not like him. But you don't know this work. You know I would like to do this for you as a favour, and you trust me when I tell you I know how to do this right. Now all you have to do is forget about this little talk, and one night you will have a phone call to say you are to spend the evening perhaps at the cricket club, some respect-able place, lots of people. Yes?'

'No,' I said. 'Listen, please. I've changed my mind. It was just an impulse. I don't want anything to happen to him at all.'

'Yes, I understand. But maybe you will change your mind again. So let me teach you how to do it properly.'

And I could see the sense in this. The plump pretty girl brought us more drinks, flirting with neither of us. And I sat and listened to Dhillon while he explained to me the proper way to do these things.

Now it's four am. Not a lot of us awake now. What about you? Are you awake? Are you often awake at four in the morning? If so, why? Is it like this with you?

* * *

190

You. Yes. What I was . . . when I was starting this, what I thought I was doing was talking to myself, trying to sort out all my stuff. For myself. But right from the start I've had a sense of you, listening to my stuff. Now she's not listening to my stuff any more, you have to listen to my stuff. If you're still listening. Strange, because I don't know who you are. I could take a line from the fat old twinkler and say it's like the dreams; you're just a part of me, like the yellow dog in the boarding house, like the tiger, like the cliffs and the sand and the rocks rushing up to meet me. But it doesn't feel like that; I don't really believe in a solipsistic universe. I think you're really there. Like the people in this story. Like . . . the Man with the Shelves. Or Mike Gibson. In one sense, of course, they're figments of my imagination, as in one sense everyone we meet is a figment of our imagination. In another sense, they were real blokes who were alive and are not alive any more. And Viola. You could say that I made her up for myself because I wanted someone I could love and who would do me harm. But in the other sense there was a real Viola, someone I could never quite capture, who was just trying to get on with her life when she was so rudely interrupted, and who couldn't, or wouldn't, finally, be what I wanted her to be.

Yes, I think you're really there. You're not Viola, because Viola doesn't listen to me any more. You're not Muriel, though I think I imagine you as somebody a little bit like Muriel. And yes, I do imagine you as a woman rather than a man. It's all right. I don't want to do you harm. I don't think that's what I want.

If I could just . . . leave it. If I could just sit still, you know? Like the man in the Harry Holland. Just sit in

191

my vest, vaguely staring at the hazy smoke in the middle distance, letting my mind go.

I don't really need to imagine atrocities. Just ordinary stuff is bad enough for a bloke like me. We had spent the evening eating swordfish and stuff and drinking wine and raki in a very pleasant little place by the castle, out on the rocks; looking out over the darkening sea, exhausting ourselves with the effort we were expending on not talking about what was happening to us. We walked back along the promenade, past the daft statue of Ataturk surrounded by his splendid young men and women tugging Turkey into the twentieth century. It was a very warm night, and there were still lots of locals parading up and down, and we walked through them slowly, holding hands; we were still very tender and solicitous with each other.

The hotel room felt very hot when we got in, and we took our clothes off and showered, separately, and lay on the bed with just the one sheet over us; and I looked at her sweet, bruised face and immediately wanted to bury myself in her again, bury my face in her, bury my prick in her, come in her and feel her coming all round me and over me and all through me; there was still part of me that couldn't believe she had stopped feeling about me the way she had felt. I started to stroke her body in all the ways I had learnt to give her pleasure, and after a while she sighed, spread her legs and said, 'Yes, all right,' and all my careful patience cracked, and I felt angry and upset, and told her how I wished she could muster up a bit more fucking enthusiasm.

'Charlie, I'm sorry,' she said. 'But that's how it is. But it's all right. I don't mind this. If you want a little fuck, it's all right.'

'You don't love me any more.' I understood it suddenly, properly, for the first time.

'I'm sorry,' she said. 'I didn't want it to be like this either.'

I looked down at my ridiculous, clownish, self-important, stupid prick and saw it dwindle and shrivel as if it was trying to get back up inside me. I felt as if I had forgotten how to breathe. I had a pain in my chest, an alarming, dangerous, physical pain; I actually felt for a moment that I was dying. There was something that my body wanted to do, and I didn't know what it was. I thought that perhaps I was going to be sick, and I stumbled into the bathroom and shut the door and crouched over the lavatory pan with my arms round it, and almost immediately started not to vomit but to sob; great, heaving, out-of-control sobs that wrenched at the muscles of my belly and my back and my chest and my shoulders. There was nothing I could do to stop this sobbing, though after a while I found that I was able to control the volume so to speak. I think this went on for quite a long time, and I can't remember exactly what I was thinking or feeling, or even if I was thinking or feeling in the ordinary sense, but I do remember the feeling that I was doing all the crying that I had ever needed to do and not done: for my mother, for my father, for Laura, for Joe, for Sal, for Viola, for myself.

'Yes, this is true. Whoever we think we are weeping for, in reality we are always and only weeping for ourselves.'

Fuck off, Fritz.

When I had got some sort of control over my limbs, I went back in the bedroom. She was lying on her side with her face to the wall. I got the bottle of raki and a pack of cigarettes and took them out on to the balcony, and sat smoking and drinking raki until it started to get light.

* * *

193

When I went inside she was sleeping. I sat on the edge of the bed for quite a long time, looking at her as she slept, as I had done so many times before. She was very brown against the white sheets, and her face looked very beautiful to me, though I knew that it was not in any ordinary sense beautiful. I loved her very much and I always felt that she could do me harm, and now she had done it. She looked very peaceful, sleeping. I was thinking quite seriously about killing her. I was not sober, of course, or anywhere near it, but my head felt hard and clear and my body felt strong. If I kill her, I thought, I'll be able to keep her like this, in my head, in my heart; she'll always be with me like this, she won't leave me. I reached out and touched her very gently, her hair . . . her throat. And she stirred a little in her sleep, and I knew I wasn't going to kill her after all. She would wake and struggle, and I wouldn't be able to bear it, seeing her terrified of me. And in any case, I loved her. I think you have to hate someone to kill them. I didn't hate her. I put both my hands round her face and she opened her eyes.

'Listen,' I said, 'I'm going out for a walk, OK?'

'Yes, all right,' she said, and closed her eyes again.

It was a beautiful morning and the promenade looked very white and clean. A cruise ship was coming into the port and I walked round to the quay to watch the people come down the gangplank and walk into the town. Some of them gave me an odd look as they passed me, seeing, I suppose, a fairly average, blokeish, middle-aged, English piss-artist who had managed to get himself crying drunk at seven thirty in the morning. None of their business. All part of life's rich tapestry.

Then I went back to the hotel, shaved, and decided to have a bath. While I was in there, Viola came in and had a piss. She looked tired and unhappy, and she didn't look at me or speak to me. She stood at the washbasin naked, brushing her teeth, and for a moment, but only a moment, I was able to see her body as just another body.

We still had two days to go.

She has moved, but I know where she is. I could pick up her scent from anywhere. She is on the top floor of this low-rise modern block and I can see her light and I can see her moving behind the curtain. Even if she looked out she wouldn't see me; it's dark here under the trees.

Getting into the building is a doddle. Up the fire escape and in through the window of the empty first-floor flat. I could go up to the top floor now, but I'm going to wait here for her. I'm going to wait here until she goes down to answer the bell. It is dark in this flat. I open the door quietly and leave it an inch or two open so that I have a clear view on to the landing. I don't know why I'm here or what I'm going to do.

I hear the bell ring upstairs, then hear her door opening. She is running down the stairs, the way she used to run to let me in – she can't wait. In a moment I'll see her. Yes, there she is; her black hair, her black skirt . . . She's pausing. She's stopped on the landing outside. She must have smelt me. I have to hold myself very still. She comes slowly towards the door. She hasn't seen me yet. She comes closer and peers through the crack, and I hear her sharp indrawn breath. Her eyes and mouth are wide. She is very frightened. I have no idea what I am about to do.

We got through the last two days with grace and style. Two invalids. Two wounded soldiers trapped in Turkey. We did quite a lot of laughing about it, as a matter of fact. And we were very tender to each other. The way I saw it: once I knew that I didn't really want to kill her, going in for ordinary meanness, bitterness, recrimination, would have been trivial and irrelevant. We spent all my money, down to the last lira, and bought each other a lot of little presents. We even managed a last, gentle, carefully negotiated fuck. I had some more crying to do, and so did she. I did mine in the early morning when she was asleep, and she did hers between midnight and two when I was asleep.

It was raining in England, and a series of accidents on the M25 made our journey very slow. We didn't talk. When we got to her place I got out to get her bag out of the boot. I was not going to be able to go in and go to bed with her. I was never going to be able to do that any more. She was going to go in alone, and I thought that the first thing she was going to do was to pick up the phone and ring the bastard that she was now in love with, the interloper, the cool shit.

She said, 'Don't let's make it painful.'
I said, 'I love you. It's all for you.'
She said, 'I know.'
Then she turned round and walked away and went into the house.

I took three or four books with me to Kusadasi, but what with one thing and another I didn't get round to reading them. I did read part of one of them, though, and last night I got it off the shelf and finished it. It's a book of short stories by a man called Italo Calvino. I guess it was the title that appealed to me: *Difficult Loves*. There was one story in particular that got to me, although it seemed at first sight to bear very little relation to the situation that I was in, or the situation that I am in. It's called 'The Adventure of a Traveler', and it describes a night spent on a train by a man who is journeying from the north of Italy to Rome to see the woman he is in love with, and his elaborate, painstaking and almost wholly unsuccessful efforts to get the compartment to himself so that he can get some sleep. The ending reads very beautifully, even in translation:

> 'He put the token in the slot, dialled the number, listened with beating heart to the distant ring, heard Cinzia's "Hello . . ." still suffused with sleep and soft warmth, and he was already in the tension of their days together, in the desperate battle against the hours; and he realized he would never manage to tell her anything of the significance of that night, which he now sensed was fading, like every perfect night of love, at the cruel explosion of day.'

The first time I read it I didn't really think about it at all: I simply embraced and identified with the feelings. The tenderness, sensuality, struggle, desperation, sadness. Yes, I thought. That's how it feels. But this bloke, Calvino I mean, not the traveller in the story, isn't really saying that. The emotions pull you that way, but he means something rather cynical: that it's better to travel than to arrive. Or to put it more grandly, that there is nothing real that is commensurate to a bloke's capacity to dream, invent, imagine. The perfect night of love is the one where you are alone, imagining her. And taken a bit further, even when you're not alone, when you're with her, you're *still* imagining her, you're still inventing her, you're still dreaming her. So reality is in our heads and nowhere else and we can't know anything or anyone except by inventing them for ourselves.

So maybe this is what he's telling me: if you had her, it was by inventing her. You can still invent her, so, if you wish, you can always have her.

* * *

It's certainly beautiful, and it may be true, but it doesn't bloody well work. Not for me. I still hurt. And now I am beginning to feel that I am permanently damaged, that I'm going to spend the rest of my life in the cruel explosion of day.

I'm going out now. Wish me luck.

I'm back.

I'm not sure what I am feeling.

In a way, it went exactly according to plan. In another way, as Dhillon warned me, it turned out to be entirely different from what I was expecting.

He sees her on Tuesdays and Fridays, and stays the night on Fridays, but not on Tuesdays – I don't know why. That meant it had to be a Tuesday. And except in particularly bad weather, he always leaves her place between half past twelve and one, and walks, or jogs, back to his place about a mile away. It's a fine night tonight.

The pick-up truck was where Dhillon said it would be. A dark grey one, a bit battered-looking. It had once had a firm's name on it, but that had been painted out. Trade plates. New tyres. I put my gloves on and tried the door. It wasn't locked. I got in and found the key where it was supposed to be, tucked into the sun visor. I started up and drove sedately round to Viola's street, which was only three minutes or so away. Parked it at the end of the road where I had a clear view up to her house. Twelve twenty-five. I lit a cigarette. My hands were steady. There was no one about at all. I could hear the traffic on the bypass half a mile away.

He came out at twelve thirty-five and crossed the road diagonally, walking quite briskly with his hands in his pockets. I started the engine but he didn't glance in my direction. I knew what he was going to do: he was going to walk through an alley which would bring him out on Park Road. Park Road is the one that skirts the little scrubby park we used to walk through to the Greek takeaway. There are lights and people on the other side of the park, even at half past midnight, but Park Road itself is a dark, quiet road, a long curving terrace on one side, the park railings on the other. Once past the park entrance, there were no more openings on that side, and there were no more alleys on the other side. I had worked out that if there was no one about I would do it there. If there were people about, there were plenty of chances further on.

When I turned into Park Road I saw him about fifty yards ahead of me, still walking briskly with his hands in his pockets. There were no other people out on the street, and I couldn't see any lights in any of the houses. I was driving on side-lights, not too fast, about twenty-five. He was walking on the pavement next to the railings and when I was about ten yards behind him I let the nearside front wheels ride up over the kerb. He looked over his shoulder then and started to turn, so that he was sideways on to me when the bumper hit him just above the knees, throwing him sideways on to the railings. All I had to do then was keep going, drop the truck off at the building site and walk home. But I didn't do that. I felt . . . cheated, I think. What I had done felt trivial and insignificant.

* * *

199

And not enough.

I parked the truck neatly at the kerb, about thirty yards on, and walked back to have a look at what I'd done. By the time I reached him, he had pulled himself up by the railings. He could stand on one leg but not the other one, and he didn't seem to be very badly hurt. He wasn't scared either; he was angry. He hadn't put two and two together yet. Not much of a mathematician after all, then.

'What the bloody hell d'you think you're playing at?' he said. 'Are you drunk or crazy or what?'

It was good that he was angry, because that made me angry too. 'Yes,' I said, and hit him hard in the face. This hurt my hand quite badly, but I think it hurt him much more. I think I broke his cheekbone. He staggered backwards and his bad leg went, and he sat down on the pavement.

'Who are you?' he said. 'What do you want?' He was beginning to understand now, and he was frightened.

'I've come to hurt you,' I said.

'Christ,' he said. His voice was high and shaky. 'You *have* hurt me.'

He was trying to get away from me, but he couldn't stand up. Realizing that it would be pointless to try to crawl away from me, he stopped, and leaned up against the railings, and resigned himself to whatever I was going to do next. It didn't seem to occur to him to yell for help. He just sat there, leaning against the railings, waiting.

I looked at him sitting there, leaning against the railings and waiting. Then I walked back to the truck, got in it and drove away. Still no one else in the street. Still no lights in any of the windows. I left the truck on the building site, with the keys tucked into the sun visor, and walked home.

* * *

I'm not sure what I feel about all this. I know it isn't enough. I know it doesn't satisfy me. I'm not going to go on and do anything else to him. I feel as if I've done that now, and it doesn't solve anything at all, as I knew it wouldn't. I am not sorry I hurt him, though, and I am not averse to the idea that he will go round in fear for quite a while, waiting for something like this, or something worse, to happen to him again. It felt good, feeling angry and hitting him. I could never feel that angry with Viola. Denial, despair, anger, bargaining, acceptance. I don't think I've ever really got beyond denial and despair, with her. Not really.

It was also rather stupid, stopping the truck and going back. It was dark in Park Road and he's never seen me before, but I should imagine that he has a pretty good idea of who I am. And when the police come round, I have a feeling that I shan't bother to deny what I did. In fact the whole thing is too irritating and trivial to think about. Except that it is better than thinking about myself, what I have become, what I am becoming.

I haven't been out of the flat for days. What day is it today? Friday. I continue to surprise myself. Last night, for example, I drank half a bottle of whisky and watched the whole of *Il Trovatore* on television, and enjoyed it very much. The surprise was nothing to do with the whisky of course. Half a bottle of whisky in an evening for me is routine carried to the point of total monotony. But opera, that's different. It's never had the slightest appeal for me, apart from Mozart; and while I felt that Viola's stricture on men who liked opera was a shade overstated, I could see what she meant. But there I was, watching this whole absurd carnival, and roaring along with it. It had Pavarotti in it, who cannot act at all and was doing the most dreadful things, taking beaming, self-satisfied curtain calls at points in the story when he was supposed to be racked with despair. But the music, and even the stark, crass subtitles that came splat splat on to the screen, were . . . The fire of love is burning in my veins. The more you love him, the more I tremble with fury. You shall have me if you wish, but cold and lifeless. Yes. Yes. They have got it right. This is what it's fucking well like. So there you are. I have become a man who likes opera. And she was wrong about men who like opera. They're not fascists, they're monsters.

It's been two weeks since I did the business on the cool mathematician, and I haven't heard anything from the police about it. There was a little item in the local paper which said that he had been knocked down by a hit-and-run driver. Nothing about a dark-coloured pick-up truck. Nothing about an assault. Odd. The only person that I could ask about it is Viola, and I don't think I could bear to see her now. No. I shall just sit here and play the Chopin Nocturnes and stare at my Harry Holland until the feeling goes away.

I sat there for a while staring at the Harry Holland, then found myself getting up, going out, getting in the car and driving round to her place. She's gone. It's empty. There's an estate agent's board outside. I . . . I can't bear the thought of not knowing where she is.

If you really had her then, you'll always have her.

No.

Sometimes, in my more lucid and sanguine moments, I have actually been able to entertain the possibility of starting again. With someone else. I imagined this young woman, walking around in the world, who didn't know me and had absolutely no idea of the kind of loving that was out here waiting for her. I imagined her having some sort of premonition; as it might be hearing a snatch of a tune that was unfamiliar but congenial, something that she might like to learn. Or catching a whiff of an unfamiliar cigarette. She might sense it in a different way, though: more like a car crash waiting to happen at an intersection. Or a shadow on her X-ray.

I've just hurt myself. I went out to get some bread and milk and stuff because it occurred to me that I hadn't really had any solid food for a couple of weeks. And on the way back in, I fell upstairs. I think I've broken my nose. Well, nothing unusual about that. Happens to people all the time, that sort of thing. It hasn't happened to me before. But what does that prove? Nothing.

Let me tell you how I like to think about her best.

She was always a strong and fearless swimmer: a much stronger and more fearless swimmer than me. She used to make me very anxious by swimming out deep when the yellow flag was up, and even when the red flag was up. This particular time I like to think about, we'd found a nudist beach in Crete that we both liked. You had to walk a long way to get to it, and scramble down some rocks, but when you got there it was good. There were never more than half a dozen other people there. One family with two little girls were often there. Sometimes another couple. There was plenty of room for all of us, and because it was a rocky beach you could find a place where no one could see you and you couldn't see anyone else.

We'd had some cheese and wine and bread, and made a little desultory, absent-minded love, and had a little sleep, and read a bit . . . I'd been reading aloud to her, a Poe story; she liked being read to. And then it was time to go in the water again. I swam out with her quite far for me, about a quarter of a mile, and we bobbed about in the water for a bit, kissing; and then she wanted to swim further out, and I floated on my back with my hands behind my head and my dick floating free, watching the clouds move across the sky. When I looked out to sea I could still just see her, her black hair appearing and disappearing over and under the small waves. I swam underwater for a little while. There were hundreds of tiny fish swimming all round me and I tried to catch one of them in my hand, but I couldn't.

When I looked out towards the horizon again, I couldn't see her at all. It was hard to propel myself high enough above the water to see very far and the waves seemed to have become a little higher. I couldn't see her anywhere. I looked back towards the shore, but I knew already that no one on that beach had a boat, and no one on that beach ever swam out even as far as I was. I thought what it would be like to lose her, never to see her again, and I thought that I couldn't bear it. I thought of swimming out myself, but that was stupid. I was such a weak swimmer compared to her, and if I did find her she would probably have to tow me back. There was absolutely nothing I could do except wait and trust that she would come back to me.

It seemed like a very long time, but it was probably only about two or three minutes before I saw her again, her dark head appearing and disappearing, and she seemed to be making no progress at all against the current; but then suddenly, she seemed to be closer, and swimming towards me quite quickly; and then I could see her all the time, and I could see her face, and she was swimming strongly and easily, and she was smiling as she swam towards me, and she swam all the way into my arms and I kissed her.

Oh, shit. Oh, shit shit shit shit shit.

I am looking in the mirror and I don't like what I see. My nose is definitely broken. I've lost a lot of weight too, in a very unappealing way: the flesh looks as if it's falling off my bones. The whites of my eyes are dirty and yellow. I seem to be growing a beard. It doesn't suit me. Well, fuck it. I'm still here, aren't I? I'm still bloody well here. Come on, then, Charlie. Give us a smile.

Christ. That was a bit of a shock. When I smiled, it reminded me of Charlie Chaplin's smile.

It reminded me of Dog Smile.

I think I'll go out for a bit now.

What I should really do, I should go and get myself a proper meal in the best restaurant that will let me in. But I'm not going to do that, because I don't feel hungry. I haven't felt hungry for quite a while.

* * *

What I think I'll do, I think I'll take a little stroll around town. And I have absolutely no idea of what I'm going to do there.

I might see you. You might see me.

I think there might be quite a few of us out there. Blokes like me.   *   *   *